LEGACY

A Traveler Series Story

Tom Abrahams

A PITON PRESS BOOK

LEGACY

A Traveler Series Story
© 2018 by Tom Abrahams
All Rights Reserved

Cover Design by Hristo Kovatliev
Edited by Felicia A. Sullivan
Proofread by Pauline Nolet
Proofread by Patricia Wilson
Interior design by Stef McDaid at WriteIntoPrint.com

tomabrahamsbooks.com

FREE PREFERRED READERS CLUB: Sign up
for information on discounts, events, and release dates:

eepurl.com/bWCRQ5

PITON PRESS

For Courtney, Luke, and Sam
You make me proud every day.

"Cowards die many times before their deaths; the valiant never taste of death but once."

—William Shakespeare

WORKS BY TOM ABRAHAMS

THE TRAVELER
POST APOCALYPTIC/DYSTOPIAN SERIES
HOME
CANYON
WALL
RISING
BATTLE
LEGACY

THE SPACEMAN CHRONICLES
POST-APOCALYPTIC THRILLERS
SPACEMAN
DESCENT
RETROGRADE

PERSEID COLLAPSE: PILGRIMAGE SERIES NOVELLAS
CROSSING
REFUGE
ADVENT

RED LINE: **AN EXTINCTION CYCLE NOVEL**

POLITICAL CONSPIRACIES
SEDITION
INTENTION

JACKSON QUICK ADVENTURES
ALLEGIANCE
ALLEGIANCE BURNED
HIDDEN ALLEGIANCE

CHAPTER 1

JANUARY 3, 2038, 3:00 AM
SCOURGE +5 YEARS, 3 MONTHS
KILLEEN, TEXAS

Lou stabbed the blade through the cover of L. Frank Baum's masterpiece. Threading the torn strip of cotton fabric through the ragged hole, she pulled it through the hole she had carved into the cover of a thick Tolstoy and knotted the ends.

"That'll do it," she said to herself. "My very own book jacket."

She chuckled at her own cleverness and slipped the veil of threaded books over her head. The thickest tomes covered her chest. The thinner ones protected her sides and back. Although it was heavier than she'd anticipated, she was certain it would do the trick. She ran her thumb across the denim blue cover of a first edition of the English version of *Lolita*.

The fourteen-year-old plucked her knives from the pressed wood tabletop where her father had spent so many days and nights reading the classics. She could hear his resonant voice in her head as he told her stories from lands and times distant from the post-apocalyptic Texas in which she lived.

She crossed the carpeted floor to the broken window that looked out toward the lake. For so long, she'd stared out at the water from the safety of the library and smiled. Now all it brought was a throbbing ache that sat low in her gut.

Lou balanced the knives in her hands and climbed through the window, careful to sidestep the shards of glass that littered both sides of the opening. Soon she was on the wide stretch of overgrown weeds that separated the building from the water.

Despite the added weight of the book jacket, she moved like a gazelle across the expanse until she found a thinning but large bottlebrush, and she crouched behind it, balancing her weight on her tiptoes. Her pulse raced, thumping at her temples and her neck, but her breathing was controlled. Her vision focused in the hazy predawn moonlight that cast a pale glow over the water.

Against the edge of the pond was the encampment of Cartel refugees. Perhaps some were Dweller defectors too. Who knew? Who cared? To Lou, they were the men who had robbed her father of their dinner and then killed him for it. There were ten of them, and they would pay. Every last one would die before the moon gave way to the sun. She owed her father that much.

Lou adjusted the jacket on her shoulders using her thumbs and took aim at her target. The men were clustered into three groups. One was between her and the water on the other side of a trio of dying hedges. One was to the left of the pond. The third was on the far side of the water near the semicircle drive that connected the property to the road. None of them, not even a lookout, was awake as far as she could tell.

Lou scanned the property and then bolted to her left toward a dry gulley that fed rainwater into the pond. There was a steep slope toward the gulley, but she maintained her footing and scurried to the base of a footbridge that crossed the dry gulley. From her spot she saw the first cluster of men. There were three of them.

She rubbed her thumbs along the knives' handles and inhaled the cool air. There was no breeze to mask her approach. She would need to be quick and precise. There was no room for error or unnecessary movements.

Lou raised herself from the gulley, the book jacket hanging and swaying beneath her chest and abdomen as she pushed up the shallow embankment. She adjusted the fall of the jacket again and bolted to the trio sleeping soundly in the pasty moonlight.

Her legs churned against the hard ground until she approached the men. Two of them were sleeping in identical positions, almost like mummies, with two feet of dewy, matted grass and weeds between them. Lou aimed for the opening, and before she reached it, she dropped her weight onto the ground and slid on her backside the final distance.

Her momentum propelled her far enough to reach the gap between the two men. As she did, she plunged both knives down at the same time, hitting each beneath their solar plexus. The knives served as brakes, and Lou's slide abruptly halted.

Both men had gasped as she stabbed them, but she'd quickly pulled the blades and finished them off much as she had the men before them. They gurgled and grunted, and one of them grasped for Lou as she rolled over him to attack the third man. His gnarled grip wrapped tightly around her wrist, yanking her awkwardly to one side. She was close enough to his face to feel the thick warmth of his breath and smell the gamey odor of the previous night's grilled squirrel.

Lou wrestled free of his weakening hold and moved to the next target. That target was now awake. He was groggy and disoriented, but he was awake. He was leaning up on his elbows, mumbling something about the noise when Lou pounced on him like a feral cat. Her attack snapped his neck backward, and his head hit the hard ground. He groaned and his eyes fluttered before Lou repeatedly drove the blades into and across the most vulnerable parts of his head and neck.

Her chest was heaving and her lungs burned from the cold air.

She rolled off the dead man and lay flat on the ground, trying to focus on the moon above to regain her center and control her heart rate. She adjusted her body against the discomfort of the sewn books pressing against the small of her back.

She closed her eyes and pictured her father. She saw his eyes peer from above the top edge of a hardcover novel. She heard the comforting crinkle of the protective clear plastic that covered the book's paper jacket.

He'd told her she was ready for this. He'd reminded her how much she'd prepared. He'd expressed pride in her unlikely strength, speed, and agility. Her slender frame and small size was an advantage, he'd said. He'd also warned her how difficult it was to take someone's life, how the act itself might get easier with time but the emotional consequence of it never did.

Lou bit the inside of her cheek to shake the thought from her preteen mind and slowed her breathing. Through her nose she inhaled and exhaled. In. Out. In. Out. In. Out. Six down. Four to go.

She rolled onto her side and looked across the pond toward the road. There was no movement where she'd last seen the four men sleeping. She could see vague shapes against the ground. They were still asleep, as best she could tell. The brief crescendo of noise from her most recent kills hadn't disturbed them.

Lou held up her blades in front of her face and turned them over in her hands. She examined them in the moonlight and then bent over to wipe them clean against the clothing of the dead men. She noticed the splatter on her book jacket and the stains on her hands. There was no wiping that clean.

Staying low to the ground and hunched over, Lou scurried closer to the quartet. She remained on the edge of the gulley until she found a squatty oak that gave her adequate cover about thirty yards from the men. Their dark, amorphous forms hugged the ground at the edge of the pond. For the first time she saw the low burning embers of a dying campfire. Threads of the orange-red glow throbbed from within the pile of sticks and twigs. There was a crude spit perched above the kindling. That was where they'd cooked her dinner. That was where they'd charred the food her father had hunted and caught. A newly familiar rush of smoldering anger welled in Lou's gut and coursed outward. Her muscles tensed; her jaw clenched; her grip on the knives tightened. Overcome with fury, she dug her foot into the dirt and leapt from behind the tree, racing toward the men. The blades swung at her sides and the book jacket swung from side to side against her body as she pumped her arms. She sprinted, reaching her top speed by the time she'd crossed the open field to the encampment. It took only seconds and she was on top of them.

She swiped and stabbed and dragged the knives at the men, blind with rage as she killed them. One. Two. Three.

But the fourth. Where was the—

"Hey," he called, his voice dry and full of sleep. He was behind her, a blanket draped over his shoulders and a shotgun in his hands.

Before Lou could react, he pulled the trigger. The twin shells rocketed from their barrels. The explosive percussion of the blast cracked through the still air as Lou felt the spray. It knocked her off balance, stunning her into inaction, and the man stepped purposely toward her. He pumped the shotgun, ejecting two shells and loading two more.

"Who are you?" he asked, aiming the barrel at her head.

Perched on her knees, Lou was already breathless. She swallowed hard and bent over at her waist, the echo of the blast ringing in her ears. She was stunned and bleeding, but she was focused enough. There was still enough anger fueling her that while she raised one hand in surrender, dropping the knife, she flung the other forward. The blade spun through the air and caught the man in his arm.

He cried out in pain and momentarily lost his hold on the shotgun. His face curled with shock, then anger, and with the blade still in him, he tried to retarget his weapon.

By then Lou had reached into her waistband, leveled the semi-auto pistol at his chest, and slid her finger onto the trigger. She applied pressure to the trigger and the gun kicked. She pulled again. And again. And again. The man spun awkwardly, dropped the shotgun, and collapsed to the ground.

Lou stood, checking the peppered holes in the books at her chest and the shallow wounds on her arms. She steadied herself, her adrenaline waning, and stepped to the dead man. She stood above him and then squatted to look into his fixed, distant gaze.

"I'm my father's daughter," she said. "His name was David. My name is Lou."

CHAPTER 2

OCTOBER 30, 2032, 7:03 AM
SCOURGE +28 DAYS
AUSTIN, TEXAS

Eight-year-old Louise held her father's hand as she watched the bodies burn. He rubbed the back of her ring finger with his calloused thumb. Neither of them spoke as the flames spread across the sheet-wrapped corpses, devouring them with thick, hungry licks.

With her free hand, Louise pinched the bridge of the surgical mask covering her nose and mouth. It didn't help. The acrid odor of burning flesh and hair stung her nostrils. She could taste it in the back of her throat, peppery and sour.

Her father cleared his throat, as if purging the taste, and wiped his eyes. Louise's eyes drifted from the growing flames and thickening smoke toward his face.

"It's not your fault," she said softly, her voice barely rising above the crackle of the fire. "You did everything you could."

He squeezed her hand but kept his sad gaze on the pyre. His voice was laced with phlegm when he spoke. "Lou, you're a good girl. Your mom loved you. So did your brother."

"She loved you too, Dad. She would tell me that all of the time when you did stupid stuff."

He chuckled with a smile that resembled a frown. "Did she?"

Lou nodded. "Davey thought you hung the moon. Mom said that too."

"Your mom used to say a lot of things," he said mournfully.

Lou turned back to the sea of flames in front of her, its heat radiating the short distance to her face. It was hot and bright, and although wisps of the smoke stung her eyes, Lou tried to keep her eyes open. In that smoke, there were flakes of her mother and her brother. Their bodies and their spirits washing toward her, sticking to her.

She and her father stood silently, only the crackle and roll of the flames filling the air between them. After what felt like an hour, but was probably only a few minutes, Lou's dad sighed raggedly.

"I should've kept Davey home from school," he said. "Then he wouldn't have gotten sick. Your mother wouldn't have—"

Holding her father's hand with both of hers, Lou squeezed. "Dad, don't."

She was eight years old. She was a second grader who liked reading and word games on her iPad. She took gymnastics three times a week and played soccer at the Y. She didn't understand what exactly the Scourge was. She didn't comprehend that two of every three people in the world would die from the pneumonic plague. She couldn't extrapolate that the rest of her life was as uncertain as the next day, the next hour.

What she did know was that school was closed and so was the gym. She understood she wasn't allowed to play with her friends or venture from their quarter-acre lot. She processed that she'd never see her mother or her brother again.

She didn't want to hear her father rewrite what had happened. In her eight-year-old mind, she had enough with which to grapple. "What ifs" were taking up space meant for other, more useful things. She was at the edge of the age of reason. Reason had no room for conjecture. Lou's father tugged on her hands with his, shaking her from the quandary.

"Come with me," he said, and led her toward the detached three-car garage, which connected to the home via a breezeway. "I need to show you something."

Watching the diminishing flames and lessening smoke of the pyre over her shoulder, Lou followed her dad into the garage. The familiar smell of engine oil, gasoline, and sawdust filtered through her mask, and she pulled it from her face, draping it at her neck underneath her chin.

Her father tugged on a pull string, and an exposed bulb snapped to life, casting a yellow glow across the part of the garage used as a workshop. He let go of Lou's hands and pushed a switch on his carpentry bench. An attached fluorescent clinked on and lit the wide table, revealing a circular table saw, a jig, and rechargeable power tools plugged into their bases. There was a bottle of Canadian whiskey to one side, it's decorative purple velvet bag cinching the oblong bottle's neck.

He wiped his hands across the table, producing a cloud of sawdust, and reached for a wall-mounted shelf above the table. With both hands, he lowered a rectangular metal box. He popped open the box and withdrew a set of keys.

Lou watched her father move deliberately from the workbench to a tall gun safe in the corner. Her eyes widened and she stepped forward into the soft spray of light to see her father unlock the safe. She'd never seen it open before.

With one hand he inserted the key, with the other he spun the combination lock from one side to the other and back again. He turned the key and pulled the handle. The door, nearly as tall as David, swung open with a heavy-sounding creak. He reached into the dark opening and removed from it a foot-long rectangular wooden box. As he turned and walked back to the workbench, his eyes held Lou where she was. He didn't have to tell her not to get any closer to the gun safe.

He reverently placed the box at the center of the workbench, as if placing an offering on an altar. With a tilt of his head, he called Lou to his side. She quickly sidled up next to him, biting her lower lip at the anticipation of what might be inside the magic box.

It was polished mahogany, stained and decorated with light-colored, decorative inlays. The hinges and delicate thumb latch were bronze. Whatever was inside the box was indeed special. Lou's pulse quickened.

He opened the box with both hands and pulled from it a yellowed, wrapped cloth that reminded her of the shrouds around her mother and brother. Slowly, he unfolded the cloth, revealing a pair of knives. He straightened them next to each other on the cloth, holding his fingertips on the handles.

"These were your great-grandfather's," he said. "They're yours now."

Lou looked up at her father, her eyes narrowed with confusion. "Mine?"

There was no hint of emotion in his response. His steely glare was as serious as she'd ever seen him.

"I won't always be here to protect you," he said. "You need to learn to protect yourself."

"With knives?"

"Guns have a shelf life," he said. "If you run out of ammunition, it's a paperweight. A knife, if properly sharpened, is a timeless weapon."

Tears welled in Lou's eyes, pooling and draining onto her cheeks. "I don't understand," she said, her chin trembling.

His glare softened and he put his hands on Lou's shoulders and knelt in front of her, pulling her into his chest. He wrapped his thick hand around the back of her head and cradled it, comforting his grieving daughter.

"I will teach you," he whispered. "You'll learn to hunt and track and cook. You'll learn how to throw knives and shoot a gun."

He backed away from her while still holding her shoulders. She was trembling and trying hard to swallow her tears. She wanted to be strong. She wanted to be tough. Her mind swirled with questions. She bit her lip to stop them from pouring out uncontrollably.

"It won't be long now until we'll lose power. We'll be on our own, Lou. Do you understand?"

She nodded her head vigorously, blinking away the tears.

"I'm not telling you this to scare you," he said, sadness seeping into his voice. "I'm telling you this so you understand what we have to do. We have to train. We have to prepare. We have to be ready. Do you have any questions?"

Lou swallowed. She ran through the litany of them in her head: *Are bad people coming for us? What will we eat? Do we have to leave our home? When can I go back to school?*

Instead of voicing those questions, she glanced at the workshop and the gleaming steel blades reflecting the fluorescent light above them. They were magnificent. She puffed her cheeks and exhaled.

"Can I hold the knives?"

Chapter 3

DECEMBER 2, 2032, 2:12 PM
SCOURGE +61 DAYS
AUSTIN, TEXAS

Lou balanced the knife in her right hand, testing its weight. She placed her index, ring, and middle finger in the middle of the handle. Her pinkie hung off the edge.

She lined up the target and took a step back and to her left. With her left shoulder facing the target, she stepped forward with her back foot. Slinging the knife as hard as she could, she held it until her arm was fully extended. Her shoulder dropped and her arm swung back across her body like a baseball pitcher.

The knife zipped through the thick, cold air and stuck deep into the trunk of the lone scrub oak tree in her backyard. No sooner had the blade sunk into the wood than she was eyeing her father for approval. He was standing to the side, his arms folded across his chest.

"Good," he said. "That's the unconventional throw. Let me see the spear style."

Lou's shoulders sank and she whined, "I'm not good at that one."

"That's why I need to see it. If you only do what you're good at, you'll never get better at anything else."

Lou rolled her eyes. "Fine."

She took the other knife and held it at her shoulder like a spear, its blade aimed at the same oak. Lou curled her tongue, took a step back, lunged forward, and hurled the knife at the tree. It hit the solid wood with a thud and dropped to the ground.

"See?" She shrugged.

David adjusted the Houston Astros baseball cap on his head and chuckled. "All right. Go get them and we'll work on it."

Lou wiped the sheen of cold sweat from her forehead with the back of her hand and trudged through the thinning grass to the tree. She picked up the failed throw and pried the good one from the tree. She wiped the blades clean and walked back toward her father.

"So your grandpa was what again?" she asked. "He did what?"

"He was in a traveling circus, Lou. I've told you this."

"I know that," she said, taking aim. "But you called it something."

She reared back and threw the knife at the tree. It hit blade first, but didn't stick.

"Not strong enough," her father said.

Lou pouted. She turned and frowned at him.

"The throw," he corrected. "Not you."

She raised the knife, blade aimed at the tree, and threw it like a spear from above her shoulder. Lou grunted as she released the knife, throwing her weight into it. The knife remained horizontal and zipped with enough speed that when it hit the oak, it stuck.

Her father applauded. "Good one. You'll get it."

Lou slunk back toward the tree. "What's it called?" she repeated. "What he did?"

"It was called the impalement arts."

Lou raised one eyebrow. "Impalement?"

David nodded. "It sounds disgusting, I know," he acknowledged. "It's a fancy-sounding name for throwing knives at people and intentionally missing them by razor-thin margins."

"Like at a circus?"

"Exactly. He worked for a traveling carnival, one of the last of its kind. He called himself El Gran Mago Cuchillo."

"The great knife magician?"

"Yes."

Lou extended her fingers and balanced the knives in her open palms. "So these were his? And he threw these at people?"

"Well, one person. Your great-grandmother."

Lou flipped one of the knives into the air above her hand and caught it by the handle. "What was her name?" she asked as she tossed it again. "El Gran Cojín Pin?"

Her father's body shook as he burst into laughter. "Too funny," he said once he'd recovered. "But no, she wasn't the Great Pincushion."

Lou's eyes danced back and forth between her hands as she flipped both knives at the same time. Each toss was a bit higher than the one before.

"Her name was Louise," he said.

She took her eyes from the knives to look at her father. Both knives hit the ground.

"Louise?"

"That's who you're named after. I honored my father's mother by naming you after her."

Lou's brow furrowed and her eyes narrowed to judgmental slits. "You know I don't like my name. Louise is such an old person's name. Luhwwwweeezzz."

"It's better than what your mother wanted to name you."

Lou squatted to pick up the knives. "Worse than Louise?"

"She wanted to name you Pearl."

Lou carefully ran her finger along the side of one blade, wiping the dirt from it. She pursed her lips. "You both were awful at names."

"You're wise beyond your years," her father said. "Eight going on seventeen. Your mother always insisted we talk to you like you were an adult. Guess she was right."

14

Lou faced the tree and readied herself to try another spear throw. She stopped and looked over her shoulder. Her father's eyes were glossy.

"You miss Momma?" she asked.

He sniffed and wiped his nose with the back of his hand. "Her and Davey," he said wistfully. "Every minute of every day, I think of them. I miss their faces, their voices, their laughter."

Lou aimed the knife at the tree and stepped into her throw. The knife flew the short distance and drilled the trunk. She closed her eyes and quickly flung the other one at the same spot. The knife stuck into the trunk less than an inch from its twin.

"It's only been a few weeks," she said. "I don't miss them yet. It feels like they're on vacation."

Lou's dad adjusted the Astros ball cap on his head and walked to the tree with his hands in his pockets, plucked the knives from their targets, and carried them back to his daughter. He handed them to her and placed his hand atop her head.

"They *are* on vacation," he said softly. "They're in paradise. They're at peace. They're laughing and singing and eating donuts."

An involuntary smile spread across Lou's face. The thought of her brother eating donuts and singing with his mouth full was comforting. It was disgusting, but it was comforting.

"We, on the other hand," her father said, "have work to do. You need to learn how to hunt and make a fire."

"We still have cans of food," she said. "And the gas stove works."

"Yes, but we're running low, we've lost power, and there's no telling how long it'll be before the gas stops working."

"I don't like cooking."

"You've never done it, so how would you know?"

"I can tell."

"There are a lot of things you haven't tried that you're going to have to like. That's just the way it is now. That is our world."

Lou sighed. Then, in a single move, spun away from her father, jumped into the air, and unleashed one of the blades. It zipped through the air, spinning quickly, and stuck into the dead center of the trunk. She landed on her feet, pirouetted, and then flung the second knife backhand at the same spot. It hit the handle of the first knife and bounced to the ground. She grunted with frustration and balled her fists.

"Almost," she said.

David, wide-eyed and slack jawed, nodded blankly. "Almost. Let's just hope you can hunt and cook as well as you can throw knives."

CHAPTER 4

"It tastes like pork," said Lou's father. "Besides, it's all we've got."

Lou sat on a gnarled, rotting log in front of the low fire her father had lit an hour earlier. She wasn't interested in the animal her dad was boiling in a pot he'd hung over the flames.

"It'll be tender," he told her. "Boiling it makes the meat fall off the bone."

An involuntary shudder rippled through Lou's body despite the radiating warmth of the fire. The idea of eating armadillo was enough to make her growling stomach go mute.

"I like rabbit better," she said. "It's meaty, like chicken."

"We won't always find rabbit."

"Even squirrel. I like squirrel."

"Squirrel tastes like pork," her father said. "Just like armadillo."

Lou waved her hand, referencing the cluster of pines and holly trees less than twenty yards from their campsite. "There are plenty of squirrels. We could eat squirrel."

Her father poked at the boiling water in the pot with a long skewer. "That's not the point of this exercise. The point is to teach

17

you about all of the different things you can eat, how to hunt them, how to clean them, how to cook them."

"I'm good with squirrels and rabbits."

Her father leaned back and smirked. "Remind me. How do you field dress a squirrel?"

Lou shifted on the log and used her hands to describe the process as she spoke. "It's pretty simple. First you flip it onto its belly and cut off the tail. Then you cut it on the sides."

"Good so far."

"Then you step on the hind end and hold the back legs. You start pulling it apart. You gotta work your fingers in there, especially at the front and back legs, but the hide comes off pretty easy."

"Then what?"

Lou wiped her nose with the back of her hand. "Then you cut off the head," she said with a chopping motion of her hands.

"What about the neck bone?"

"Snap it with your fingers," she said. "Cutting through bone with a knife dulls the blades."

"Good."

"If it's a boy, you have to—"

"You can skip that explanation."

"Okay." Lou giggled. "After…that…you pinch the stomach and cut into it so you can take out the guts. You gotta be careful there, because if you slip up with the knife, you can spoil the meat."

"Correct."

Lou made cutting motions with her hands. "Then cut out the entrails. Check the liver. It needs to look healthy. If it's not, you don't want to eat the meat."

"Nice."

"Then you make little cuts at the wrists and ankles and snap off the feet. Then you're ready to cook it."

"Excellent," said Lou's father. "You have a good memory. Now, you saw the armadillo wasn't all that different. Same principles apply, though you need to cut the fat from underneath the front and back legs. You can cook it in the shell or not. We're boiling it, so I took it out of the shell."

Lou made a face like she smelled something sour. "The whole idea of eating something in a shell is just gross."

"Gross? You've eaten shrimp. You've eaten crab. You love lobster."

Lou shook her head. "That's different."

Lou's dad shook his head in frustration and stood to check the armadillo. His face was above the pot, steam swirling around his head. He inhaled what Lou was certain was a disgusting aroma and poked the skewer around the inside of the pot. He looked over at her with a wide grin. "It's getting close," he said. "You ready to pitch the tent?"

Lou nodded and pushed herself from the log. Her legs were stiff and she stretched, arching her back and raising her arms above her head. She suppressed a yawn.

"How long is this trip?" she asked. "As long as the last one?"

David shrugged. "Each one is different. To be honest, Lou, I make them up as I go. I've got in my head all of the things I want you to learn. I teach them to you as they come to me."

"So, three days?"

He laughed, leaned the skewer against the side of the pot, and walked over to Lou. He grabbed one end of the tent and helped her shake it loose.

"Maybe longer," he said. "The weather is good. There are plenty of critters out here to hunt. Why are you asking? Do you have somewhere else to be?"

Lou crouched to lay the tent corners on the ground so she could slide a flexible rod inside the loop at the edge of the tent's frame. She fumbled with the rod but managed to fit its end into the loop. "I still don't get why all of this is so important," she said. "We have a house. We have a garden."

David slid a rod inside his side of the tent, creating a nice, clean arc along the edge of the four-person tent. He worked silently until he had the frame completed.

Lou finished her side and took a metal stake from the tent's backpack container. She wiggled the tip of the stake into the ground and then found the small rubber mallet clipped to the outside of the tent's pack. A couple of strong whacks drove the stake into the ground.

"I've told you this before," he said. "We won't always have our home, Lou. It's been three months since…since the world changed. That's a blip."

Lou moved to the other corner on her side of the tent and shoved a second stake into the dirt. She flipped the mallet around in her hand and then whacked it several times. But the ground was too hard, and she couldn't drill the stake deep enough.

She clenched her jaw and smacked the stake harder and harder. It didn't budge. She grunted in frustration and whacked the stake a half dozen more times before her father stopped her.

He knelt beside her and put his hand on her back. "You need help?" he asked softly.

"No," Lou snapped. She raised the mallet above her head and slammed it onto the spike. Then she pounded it until beads of sweat bloomed along her hairline and she was nearly out of breath.

"Are you finished?"

Lou shot a look at her father, hoping it would convey to him how upset she was. She wanted him to know she wasn't angry at the spike. She was angry at the thought she'd have to leave her home.

He held out his hand. "Let me try. I'll get it started, and then you can finish it. We haven't had rain in a while. The ground is really hard in spots."

Lou reluctantly handed over the mallet and inched away from the spike. Her father whacked at it until it dug deeper into the earth by a few inches. Then he offered the mallet back to Lou.

"It's fine," she said. "You finish it."

He jabbed the mallet toward her. "No, you finish it. It's important."

"Why?" she snarked. "Because we have to leave our house?"

"Look, we're not leaving today. Probably not tomorrow or the next day. But soon enough, we'll run out of supplies. We'll need to head out and find somewhere else to settle. I don't like it either, Lou. But you're old enough to understand the gravity of the situation."

Lou's scowl softened into confusion. "What does that mean? Gravity?"

"It means it's serious. I know you're eight years old. You should be in school, running around on the soccer field or doing flips in the gym. You should be torturing your brother or disobeying your mom. You should be learning about the planets and reading Clifford books."

"Clifford is for babies."

"You get my point," he said. "You have to grow up sooner than you should. You have to be ready to provide for yourself, to understand this is a dangerous world filled with dangerous people. You're smart enough to get it. I don't like it any more than you do. But that's how it is, and I would be a terrible father if I didn't tell you the truth."

Lou thought about Clifford the Big Red Dog. She secretly liked him. She couldn't admit it, but she did. She liked *Goodnight Moon* too and *A Is For Astronaut*. There was something comforting about their simplicity and implicit happiness. The world was bathed in light when she read those books and was far different from the gray and sepia that had settled over her real existence.

Lou knew the time for childish things had passed. She was eight going on seventeen. She stood up, handed her father the mallet, and brushed off her pants.

"You're a good dad," she said, rubbed the dirt from her hands, and walked over to the pot. She inhaled the gamey aroma filtering through the steam from the boiling pot.

While her father finished hammering in the two remaining stakes, she poked at the armadillo with the skewer. The tines dipped into and out of the meat easily, and she called over her shoulder, "It's done. I'm ready to eat."

CHAPTER 5

SEPTEMBER 25, 2033, 5:56 AM
SCOURGE +11 MONTHS, 23 DAYS
AUSTIN, TEXAS

Lou's eyes popped open. A sheen of sweat dampened her neck and back, and her pulse was racing. Another bad dream, in a year full of them, had kept her from a restful night of sleep. But it wasn't the nightmare that awakened her. It was a noise coming from downstairs. She wondered if the clanging was part of her dream. Then she heard it again, a loud bang followed by hushed voices.

She rolled onto her side, the morning chill sending a shudder along her spine. Her shirt was stuck to her back. She nudged her father.

"Dad," she whispered.

He was on his side, facing her. He slept with a pout on his face as if everything in his subconscious was worrisome. He didn't react, so she shook his shoulder and whispered more forcefully. Another noise filtered into the room from downstairs.

"Dad," she said, "get up."

He opened one eye and then the other. "What?" he asked groggily.

"There's somebody in the house."

23

His eyes widened and his focus sharpened. He turned his head to listen and then sat up straight, shrugging the sheet and blanket to the foot of the bed. He shook his head. "I don't hear—"

Another clang stopped him short. He sprang from the bed and drew his index finger to his lips. Lou slid from the bed onto the floor. She padded quietly to her father's side as he neared the closed bedroom door. Across the door was a long metal bar, the kind used to keep sliding doors closed. Her father had altered it to work as an extra barricade.

He raised the bar until it sat vertically along the wall adjacent to the door at its hinges, pressed one hand to the door, and gripped the knob. Slowly, purposefully, he cracked open the door and peered through the thin opening. He stood there for a moment, then quietly backed away from the door and closed it again, turning the knob slowly to keep it from making a loud noise.

He crouched down and put his hands on Lou's elbows. "There are three people down there," he whispered. "Maybe more."

Lou searched his face for comfort, for reassurance they'd be fine. Instead, he offered steely determination. His strong jaw set and he looked past her toward the large dresser next to the bed. He stood, rubbed Lou's head, and moved across the room. From the top dresser drawer, underneath a pile of socks, he removed a Smith & Wesson .38 Special double-action revolver. He opened the cylinder and checked it. He shook it closed and handed it to Lou.

"This is an insurance policy," he told her. "Remember what you've practiced."

Lou took the pint-sized weapon in her delicate but skilled hands and felt its heft. She'd fired the weapon countless times in the backyard, and although she wasn't as accurate as she was with a knife, she could handle the smaller pistol without a problem, and she always shot a tight pattern into the paper targets her dad pinned to the weary scrub oak.

The pulse throbbing in her neck and her heartbeat quickening in her chest, Lou drew slow, deep breaths through her nostrils in an attempt to even her keel. Her palm was sweaty against the .38's molded grip. She rubbed her thumb along the inscription on the matte silver finish underneath the cylinder. MADE IN USA, it read.

Lou's dad had disappeared inside the dark space of his walk-in closet and emerged with his Mossberg AR-15 5.56. Lou thought it mean looking: an all-black tactical semiautomatic version of the weapon that held more than two dozen rounds.

It was lightweight. She'd fired it, too, but wasn't as proficient with the five-pound rifle pulled snug into her shoulder as she was with the fifteen-ounce pistol extended in front of her and held tight with two hands. He'd taught her how to fire a rifle using a Ruger 10/22, the same easy-to-use weapon her Dad had learned to fire as a Boy Scout. It was a different animal than the AR-15.

He shoved the mag into the bottom of the rifle, pulled back the charging handle to chamber a round, and walked past Lou to the door. He looked over his shoulder and stopped with his hand hovering above the knob.

"You bolt this door behind me," he said. "Lock it. Pull down the bar. Do not open the door for anyone other than me. You hide in the closet and keep the gun aimed at the door. Got it?"

Lou started to complain. A knot swelled in her throat. Her chin quivered. Yet she nodded and obeyed orders. Her father dipped through the door, and she closed it behind him.

She pulled down the bar, wiggled it to make sure it was snug, and backed away. She scurried to the closet and tiptoed into the dark, closed the door, and slowly backed her way to its rear wall. She slid onto her heels and squatted in the darkness in her bare feet and thin pajamas. Hiding among the drape of long-sleeved shirts and suits her father no longer wore, she wiped her sweaty palms on her cotton pants and listened to herself breathe. She wasn't there long.

She strained, trying to hear what, if anything, was happening downstairs. The thick knot in her throat ached. The more she tried to listen to her father confront the intruders, the more she was distracted by that ache and the throb of her pulse in her ears.

Lou scrambled to her feet and stepped forward. She burst from the closet and strode to the bedroom door. She pressed her ear against it just as a burst of gunshots rang out. Her body shuddered from the surprise as another quick volley echoed through the house.

Lou slung open the bar and swung open the door. Her hands trembling, but tightly gripping the pistol, she inched forward into the hallway. A long balustrade ran along one side of the hall, giving a partially obstructed view to the first floor and the edge of the kitchen. There was the distinctive shrill of a crying child.

Her father was there, his back to her. He was standing, exposed, with the rifle to his shoulder. Its barrel was leveled at something. He kept shifting his aim from right to left and back again. Lou crouched at the balustrade, pressing her face to the wrought-iron spindles, trying to get a better look at the intruders.

She wanted to call to him. She wanted to ask him if he was okay. She wanted to jump from the second floor and stand at his side, fending off the enemy.

She stayed quiet. Watching.

"C'mon now," her father called. He waved the Mossberg toward the front door of the house, which was behind him and to his left. "Let's go. Take what you have in your hands and go."

He stepped backward toward the bottom of the staircase, keeping the weapon trained at the kitchen, shifting it from side to side at whatever unseeable threats lurked beyond Lou's sight line.

Then she saw them. First the man appeared from the kitchen. His arms were raised above his head, a large steak knife gripped tightly in his left hand. He wore a wool cap and a navy colored barn jacket. His eyes were sunken and desperate. The rest of his face was hidden behind a thick, wiry beard that sprang from his cheeks as if a cloud of static electricity followed him wherever he went.

Next to appear was a woman. She was taller than the man and

thinner. Her clothes hung on her like an adult's would a child. Her pants were cinched tight at her nonexistent waist, and her long, bony fingers were clutching cans of food, holding as much as she could carry against her body. A thin gold band hung loosely above the knuckle on her left ring finger.

Lou bit her lip to prevent herself from screaming at the woman for stealing her food. Unlike the man, whose eyes were fixed on her father, the woman kept her vacant gaze at the floor. Her chin was tucked against her chest above the canned soup and pasta. Her shoulders caved inward in shame.

Tagging along at the woman's heels and holding on to the back of her loose pant leg was a child. Lou couldn't tell if the shaggy, filthy kid was a boy or a girl. She imagined he or she was her age or younger. The child was whimpering, tears streaking down reddened cheeks.

Lou's father kept the rifle trained at the child as the trio passed him and reached the wide-open front door. They trudged out and Lou's dad followed them to the threshold. He called after them, warning them not to come back. He told them he wouldn't be as generous the next time. He slammed the door shut and leaned against it with a flat palm. The Mossberg hung at his side.

"Dad?" Lou said, her voice more of a scratchy squeak than anything else. "What just happened?"

His neck snapped to the side and he swung around to face her. His face was etched with an odd combination of exhaustion and fear. He suddenly looked years older. His hair was grayer. The brightness in his eyes, which had been waning since the Scourge cut their family in half, was muted. There were deep furrows digging along the sides of his cheeks and around his mouth. They matched the parallel rivers of lines that stretched across his broad forehead.

"What are you doing there?" he asked in a clipped, irritated tone. "I told you to stay in the closet with the bedroom door barricaded."

She couldn't explain what had compelled her to leave the relative safety of the bedroom closet other than to tell him she was worried about him. She stared at her father awaiting an answer to her question.

He glared at her for a moment, peered through the peephole in the front door, and ran his free hand across the top of his head. He looked up at Lou and sighed. The worry lines in his face relaxed somewhat, and he climbed up the stairs toward his daughter. He carried the Mossberg in one hand and slid the other along the cherry-stained bannister as he ascended the steps. By the time he'd reached the landing, Lou had flung herself at him and wrapped her arms around him. She was still holding the Smith & Wesson .38.

"They wanted food," he said. "Nothing else."

Lou tilted back her head and looked up at her dad. "But the gunshots—"

"I fired off a few rounds to scare them," he said. "I didn't hurt anybody."

"Why did you let them take our food?"

"They were desperate. Desperate enough to break into someone's house and risk their lives for cans of soup."

"But they took our food," she said. "They stole from us."

He bent onto one knee and laid the Mossberg on the floor. "We'll be fine. We can take care of ourselves. We have skills; they don't."

Lou frowned. "They weren't very smart about it."

"If all crooks were smart, cops would never catch anybody."

"Where are the cops now?"

"We're the law," her father said. "We protect what's ours. We decide, using our own morals, what's right and wrong. If you do what your heart tells you is right, you won't ever regret what you do."

"It would have been right to kill them," said Lou. "They came into our house. They stole our food. That man even took a knife."

"Look," said her father, a hint of sparkle returning to his eyes, "we showed them mercy. We did a good thing. There is enough bad right now. A little good doesn't hurt anything."

Lou studied her father's face. She couldn't tell if he actually believed what he was telling her. It didn't matter. He wanted *her* to believe it. She didn't. She believed the man would come back.

She was right.

The intruder waited a week before he came back. On his return surprise visit, he didn't bring the woman or the child. And her father wasn't as merciful.

CHAPTER 6

OCTOBER 1, 2033, 10:32 PM
SCOURGE +11 MONTHS, 30 DAYS
AUSTIN, TEXAS

Lou was reading in the candlelight. The yellow flicker and faint scent of lavender cascaded across the family room. Her father was in his favorite chair, a replica Eames with brown synthetic leather on the high-back seat and matching ottoman. His eyes were closed and his fingers were laced together at his chest.

He'd never napped before the Scourge. He'd been an IT specialist with the Texas Department of Transportation. He'd worked ten hours a day, five days a week. He'd drive straight to pick up Lou at gymnastics or the Y, toss the ball with Davey, and sit and watch romantic comedies with his wife. He'd read aloud to both children before bed.

Soon, though, his love of books was surpassed by his daughter's. Lou was reading simple, monosyllabic words at age four. She could breeze through Dr. Seuss at five. In second grade, she was reading at an eighth-grade level. David would sit proudly on the edge of her bed, his back against the headboard, watching her breeze across pages with her finger guiding her from one word to the next. Now he frequently napped while she read, using her escape to embrace his own.

She occasionally took stock of him, looking up from the pages of Suzanne Collins's seminal dystopian trilogy to check whether or not he'd awoken from what had swollen into a four-hour nap. Lou couldn't put down the book, even though she didn't understand all of the vocabulary or why the world was the way it was. She was entranced by the main character, a young girl powerful enough to forge her way through the apocalypse. Unlike Lou, the main character still had a mother and a sibling. Other than that, she could imagine herself wielding a crossbow and fighting to the death. She skipped the parts with kissing.

As she flipped from one chapter to the next, pausing to catch her breath, a flash of movement across her peripheral vision caught her attention. She glanced up, looking at her dad. He was motionless except for the rhythmic rise and fall of his chest.

She scanned the room, searching the dull edges of the light where it blended into the darkness. She glanced from her comfortable seat in the corner of the sofa toward the window at the front of the house. The blinds were pulled, but the slats were open. Nothing.

Lou sighed a little-girl sigh and returned to the book. She flipped up the dog-ear at the top of the page and ran her finger down the page to find her spot. She'd only started the third paragraph of the new chapter when she saw the flash again.

It was coming from outside. She was sure of it. Despite its suddenly magnetic pull, Lou avoided looking at the window. She slowly closed the book and leaned to her side to set it on the coffee table in front of the sofa and blew out the candle, bathing the room in darkness.

She waited for a moment for her eyes to adjust; then she rolled to the floor and crawled the short distance to her father. She eased up beside him and shook him awake.

"There's someone here, Dad," she said. "I've seen them through the window."

Her father sat still, as if he hadn't heard her. He reached out and gently wrapped his fingers around her forearm and whispered to her, "Get upstairs."

Lou followed his instructions and started making her way to the stairs. She was on all fours, crawling across the floor. Behind her, she could hear her father checking his Mossberg. He'd kept it with him every minute of every day during the past week.

Lou started to climb the steps but stopped and looked over her shoulder. Through the blue-gray, lavender-scented darkness, she could see her father inching his way to the window. He was squatting with the rifle in both hands. There was nothing outside the window as far as Lou could see, but her mind pictured the intruder and the knife he'd carried from their home.

She hurried up the stairs and along the hallway to the bedroom. Once inside, she flung herself onto the unmade bed and reached under her stack of down pillows. She felt the twin grips of her beloved knives and pulled them out from under the pillows. Tucking them into her matching leather sheaths at her waistband, she hurried back to the hallway. Disobeying her father, she grabbed the finial at the corner of the balustrade and used the banister to guide her back down the stairs. When she reached the first step, she stubbed her toe and stumbled into the railing. She caught herself before she fell face-first onto the floor, but the noise was enough to wake the dead.

Lou's father swung around, stood, and took two deliberate strides toward Lou, aiming the weapon at her. The weapon was pulled tight to his shoulder, the barrel leveled at her chest.

"It's me," she squeaked. "It's me, Dad."

He lowered the weapon and cursed. "Sheesh, Lou," he exclaimed in a forced, hushed voice. "I thought I told you to get up—"

The window breaking at the back of the house sounded like the clink of ice cubes in a glass. Lou's father weaved his way past the furniture to his daughter's side and put his hand on the small of her back.

If someone could make a whisper sound like a scream, he'd perfected the skill. Even in the relative darkness, Lou could see his face was red. "Get upstairs now," he spat through clenched teeth.

Lou bounded up the steps two at a time, stopping only when her father whispered her name. She looked down at him, her hands white-knuckling the knives in her hands.

"I love you," he said. "Know that above all else."

"I love you too," she said, and her father disappeared past the steps toward the back of the house. There was a bedroom, an office, and a laundry room that connected the kitchen to the covered walkway between the house and the garage.

Lou took a beat and measured her nerves. She eyed the top of the steps, then craned her neck back toward the bedroom where her father wanted her to hide.

Everything in her gut told her not to hide, not to run from whatever was coming into their home. Her father had been lucky the first time. She didn't have confidence this second intrusion would end without violence.

Against her father's stern warning, she descended the steps to the first floor again. Her curiosity was as acute as her bravery. One step at a time, she moved swiftly through the house to find her father and the coming threat. If anyone had an advantage in the dark, it would be them. No matter how many bad people were coming, none of them knew the layout of the house like they did.

Lou stood at the bottom of the stairs for a beat, then followed her father's path to the first-floor back hallway. She'd taken three or four steps toward the bedroom when she heard shouting and then a pair of gunshots coming from the office. Twin flashes strobed into the hallway. Her father had fired the Mossberg.

Lou pulled the knives from her waistband and bounded toward the fray as another flash lit her path for an instant. There was more shouting and the sound of a struggle as she found the doorway to the office. It was dark and Lou could only make out the vague shapes of two figures wrestling each other. Or was it three? She couldn't tell.

Beyond the struggle, the large window was shattered and the blinds were askew, if not ruined. Lou adjusted the grip on her knives. She couldn't tell which of the men was her father. It was too dark.

She started to call out to him, but when she opened her mouth, one of the figures lifted his head, creating a faint silhouette against the window behind him. In that instant, Lou raised her right hand, turned her shoulder, and zipped the knife at the man's neck.

It was the first time she'd thrown her knife at a person. She hit her target. Even in the darkness, Lou saw the man jerk at the impact of the blade and reach for it. He stumbled away from the fight and fell back against her father's wall desk before crashing to the floor.

"Lou," her father grunted, continuing to fight with the remaining intruder. He raised his hand as the attacker slammed him to the floor on his back.

With adrenaline coursing through her, Lou slid the other knife from her left hand to her right and, in a single fluid motion, moved from the doorway and jumped onto the attacker. While he fought to fling her from his side and back, she jammed the knife into his ribs. The man screamed and grabbed for her. She could feel the knife hitting the bones and drove it deeper into his body before he successfully bucked her off. She fell back, hitting her head on the wooden leg of a recliner in the corner. Her head rattled and her vision blurred for an instant, but she quickly regained her wits, realizing she still had the knife in her hand. She rolled over onto her stomach and dove back onto the wailing attacker at the same time her father managed to pull the man onto the floor, gathering him in a headlock.

Lou slammed the knife into the man's right thigh near his groin, aiming for the inside of the thigh like her dad had taught her. The man, whose struggle was weakening, kicked his legs once and then spasmed. His body went limp and his thick hands slapped to the floor. The room fell quiet except for the heavy breaths puffing from Lou and David. He shoved the man aside and crawled toward Lou. She lunged at him, wrapping her arms around his sweaty neck.

"Are you okay?" he asked.

Lou nodded emphatically. "You?"

"Yeah. I'm fine."

Lou expected him to scold her for not obeying, for not remaining in the locked bedroom, as he'd repeatedly instructed her to do. But he didn't. He held her for the longest time. Lou squeezed her eyes shut and adjusted her wrap around her father's neck, attaching herself in a way that she hoped told him not to let go. She couldn't bear to look at what she'd done.

CHAPTER 7

OCTOBER 2, 2033, 9:16AM
SCOURGE +1 YEAR
AUSTIN, TEXAS

There were already flies buzzing in and out of the broken window, and the office held an almost imperceptible faint odor that was both sour and nauseatingly sweet. Lou's gaze washed over the three dead bodies that littered the office floor. She recognized one of them as the man who'd broken into their home a week earlier. The others were strangers.

One of the strangers was sitting awkwardly against the wall underneath the window amidst the shards of window glass that decorated the floor. His eyes were fixed and opaque, his jaw hung open, and his shirt was painted with his own blood. There was a pair of tightly spaced holes in the center of his chest, from which a trail of dark, dried blood led to his waist. His grungy, torn cargo pants were soiled. The rubber soles of his shoes were worn through underneath the big toe, providing windows to the thinly calloused balls of his feet.

"I got him as he came through the window," said Lou's dad. He stood behind her in the doorway, both of them having wandered downstairs for the first time after a restlessly uncomfortable night's sleep.

Lou stared at the man's lifeless expression, unable to turn away despite the sting of bile rising in her throat. "I heard the shots."

David pointed at the thin man crumpled next to the wall desk. The ragged puncture on his neck was the width of the blade that killed him. He was sopped in his own blood, which had leached across the floor and formed a macabre pool, bathing the dead man. There were cuts across his knuckles, the backs of his hands, and along his forearms.

"He's the same guy who was here before," said Lou's father. "He must have been the one who broke the window."

Lou stood motionless, transfixed by the fatal wound she'd inflicted. A fly landed on one ragged edge of the cut, rubbed its legs together, and skipped to the other edge. Lou followed the insect as it jerkily moved again and then flew in a looping pattern through the room and out the window. Her father's voice interrupted her trance.

"He must have been waiting for me," he said. "He might have heard me coming, because as soon as I hit the office doorway, I saw the guy coming through the window and opened fire. Next thing I knew, I was on the floor, fighting to keep the rifle in my hands."

He pointed past the third body to a bullet-sized hole in the far wall. "He got it from me. Then he had me in a bad way. You saved me, Lou."

He squeezed her shoulders and she raised her hands to place them on his. She didn't say anything. She didn't know what to say. Even precocious nine-year-olds don't always have the right words. A fly buzzed past her and circled back to the dead men.

"We're going to need to leave," said her father. "It's not safe here anymore."

Lou pulled away from him and spun around to face him, craning her neck back as far as she could to look at him. The confusion and fear on her face must have been evident.

Her father's eyes glistened and he swallowed hard. "We've been broken into twice now. It's just the beginning."

"But he's dead," Lou said. "He can't come back again."

"True. But others will come. Who knows how many he, or his wife, told about our home. When he doesn't return to wherever it is he came from, there'll be people looking for him. It's only going to get worse, Lou. As much as I want to stay here, we can't."

Lou's stomach churned and her mouth went dry.

This was the only home she'd ever known. It was where her family of four had lived for the entirety of her life. It was where half of her family had died. Their ashes were scattered amongst the oleander and daylilies in the backyard by the fence. She could still go into her brother's bedroom closet, stand among his hanging clothes, and remember how he smelled like sweat and Hill Country dirt.

The house was the last vestige of normalcy. Without it, they'd be more than homeless; they'd lack a center. Their universe would wobble and spin unevenly forever through the darkness of the post-apocalypse.

Still, as she looked over her shoulder at the bodies, she believed her father was right. He had to be right. He was her dad, and even if he'd been wrong to send her to the room and lock the door, he was bound to be right about this.

Wasn't he?

She sucked in a breath laced with uncertainty, drew it into her tiny lungs, held it there, and then exhaled slowly through her nostrils. She looked back up at her dad.

"Okay," she said, her feet still cemented to the floor. "If you say so."

He smiled weakly and rubbed his hand on her head. He stepped past her and into the room. Near the desk, he found his Mossberg and bent over to pick it up, then bent down again and retrieved his Astros ball cap. He started to put it on his head but glanced over at Lou.

"Your hair's a mess," he said.

"Because you messed it up."

He smirked, awkwardly trying to lighten the mood, and tossed her the cap. "Try this."

She caught it and put it on her head. It was too big and came down over her eyes, so while her father searched the room for anything else worth taking, she adjusted the sizing strap on the back of the cap and slid it back atop her head. She ran both hands along the bill and pulled down, to curve it, as she'd seen her father do every time he donned the blue cap embroidered with a white *H* atop an orange star.

The bill still hung low above her eyes, so she spun the cap to the side and tucked her hair up under it. "What do you think, Dad?"

He crossed the room, stepping over a body, and smiled genuinely. He reached her, holding the Mossberg at his side, and gripped the top of her head with his free hand. "I think it's yours now," he said. "A little piece of home to take with us."

Lou's heart fluttered, and the emptiness that had racked her gut when he'd told her they'd have to leave was somewhat filled. Lou followed her father from the room. He explained there was a lot of work to do, especially given that he planned to leave by the next morning.

CHAPTER 8

OCTOBER 10, 2033, 5:44 PM
SCOURGE +1 YEAR, 2 DAYS
MARBLE FALLS, TEXAS

"So we still don't know where we're going?" asked Lou. The sun was low on the horizon, casting long shadows at her. She was facing west, her hands on her hips. Her legs were jelly after another long day of walking.

"Not yet," said her dad.

She faced her father, who was sitting on a park bench. "How far did we walk today?"

"Seven miles. Same as yesterday."

She stepped across some thick tree roots protruding through the thinning grass and plopped down on the bench beside him. He was adjusting his socks, doubling them over to lessen the pain of the blisters that he'd been complaining about for two days.

They were in an abandoned RV park at the foot of a bridge that stretched across the Colorado River on Highway 281. There were a couple of rusting homes on wheels still hitched to their posts. The rest of the place was empty. They hadn't seen anyone in a couple of miles.

"It's been a week, right?" she asked.

"Eight days," he said.

"So what day is it?"

Her father squeezed his eyes shut in thought then nodded. "I guess it's Monday," he said with a lilt that made him sound less than certain. "I think it's Monday."

"What town are we in now?"

"Marble Falls."

"What's in Marble Falls?"

He slid his shoe back onto his foot and tied the laces into a double knot. "We are."

"C'mon, Dad," she whined. "What's here? What's special?"

"What's with all of the questions? Normally you wait until it's time to go to sleep to pepper me with questions."

Lou shrugged. "I don't know. I just like it when you tell me special things about the places we visit."

Lou's father rubbed the thickening scruff on his chin and leaned his elbows on the back of the bench. He pinched the bridge of his nose and exhaled. "Well, I think the most interesting thing about Marble Falls is that in 1917, the town elected the first woman mayor in the state."

Lou cocked her head with interest. "What was her name?"

"Birdie Crosby."

"Birdie?"

"It was a nickname."

"Weird nickname."

"What was weird," he said, "was that she got elected when women couldn't vote."

"What does that mean?"

"It means that a long time ago, only men could vote. Women weren't allowed."

Lou furrowed her brow. "That's stupid. Women are smarter than men anyhow."

Her dad chuckled. "Oh yeah?"

Lou nodded. "Mom used to say that. She used to say women were good at doing things, and men were good at arguing about how to do them."

"That's funny," he said, "because your mother, as much as I loved her and still do, could start an argument in an empty house. She was a feisty one."

"Feisty?"

"Determined. Spirited."

"Am I feisty?"

"Yes. You're feisty."

"Do you think women are smarter than men?" she asked. "Be honest."

"I think you're smarter than me. Is that a good enough answer?"

"That answer tells me you're smart," said Lou. "But I already knew that."

"Gee, thanks."

"How long are we staying here?" she asked.

"Just the night." Her father shrugged off his pack and set it on the ground in front of him. "I think I better go check the pair of trailers over there before we get too comfortable."

He checked his Mossberg to make sure it was ready to fire. He pulled back the charging handle and saw the round in the chamber. He released it and pushed the mag to make sure it was fully seated. He motioned for Lou to stay put while he marched toward the two remaining mobile homes.

With the rifle pulled to his shoulder, clicked off the safety, and swept the barrel in short moves to the right and left as he approached the first of the homes, a silver Airstream trailer replete with large dents across its reflective surface. When he reached the door, he banged on it with the barrel and stepped back. No answer. He knocked again with no response. He swung open the door and disappeared inside the trailer.

Lou looked over one shoulder and then the other, making sure she was still alone. One hand slid onto the knife handle tucked at her waist.

Moments later, her father emerged hurriedly from the trailer, a sour look on his face as he stumbled away from the open doorway, coughing. He slapped the door closed again.

"Dead cats," he called out to Lou. "Awful smell."

Lou nodded. Her nose crinkled reflexively as if the pungent odor had traveled across the park.

Her father moved to the adjacent plot, which housed a double-wide elevated on cinder blocks. Its pale-yellow aluminum siding was peeling at the corners, and rust trimmed the windows. Before he stepped onto the cast concrete steps leading up to its door, he looked over at Lou. "You okay?"

Lou nodded. "Yes," she said. She didn't tell him she didn't like the idea of him going anywhere without her.

He smiled faintly and then bounded up the steps and banged on the door with the butt of the Mossberg. He stepped off the concrete stoop and back down a step, keeping his aim at the door.

Lou stood up when she saw the door crack open. She pulled the knife from her waist and flipped it around in her hand. Her father backed down another step.

"I'm here with my daughter," her father said. "My name's Dave. My daughter is Lou."

Lou took a couple of steps forward. She hadn't taken off her pack yet. It hung heavy on her shoulders as she moved carefully toward her father.

"We're just passing through," he said. "Don't want any trouble."

Lou had split the distance between the bench and her father when twin shotgun barrels and a head peered past the edge of the open door. Lou stopped, balancing on the fronts of her toes.

The shotgun was aimed at her father, but the head turned and faced Lou. It wasn't what the girl expected. Looking at her through Coke-bottle glasses and from underneath a gray wig was a grandmotherly-looking woman with a road map of wrinkles on her face and Chiclet dentures in her mouth.

"Come here," the woman said to Lou. "Let me see you up close."

Lou stayed put and looked to her father for guidance. He glanced at the woman and then back at Lou to give her a tacit nod of approval. She leaned into her first step and slowly, deliberately moved close to her dad.

The woman, whose voice warbled when she talked, waved the gun at her. The oversized shotgun dwarfed the slight woman and looked heavy enough to topple her over, but she handled it with apparent skill.

"Is that a knife in your hand?" she asked. "And another at your waist?"

Lou glanced again at her father before nodding at the woman. She tightened her grip on the knife.

"What's a little thing like you doing with big knives like that?" The woman poked the barrels at Lou's dad. "You so afraid of the Cartel you got your baby girl carrying knives?"

"Cartel?" he echoed.

The woman's brow shot up toward her false hairline, her eyes bulged with shock, and her mouth opened as wide as the Chiclets would allow. She lowered the shotgun and motioned toward the inside of her home.

"Put your gun down, Dave," she said. "You need to come in here and learn some things."

Lou's father hesitated, but lowered the Mossberg and followed the woman into her trailer. Lou hurried up the steps, still gripping the knife in her right hand, and stood inside the doorway.

The home was dark and smelled like mildew. The woman was already across the length of the sitting room and had found a spot in a plush rocking chair. She held the shotgun across her lap.

Across from the chair was a love seat covered in a knitted afghan. Lou and her dad sat next to each other, both sinking into the aged foam seats.

"I don't know where you've been, Dave," said the woman, "but the whole reason I got this shotgun ready to go is the Cartel. Not that it would do me any good. Those boys want something, they figure out a way to take it. A blind old bat like me ain't gonna rightly stop them."

She adjusted herself in the chair and rocked back, using the balls of her bare feet to move back and forth.

"Is it a gang?" asked Lou's dad.

"More like a bunch of gangs all rolled into one," she said. "You sure you ain't heard tell of 'em?"

"No. We haven't."

"Well, it's like all of the bad folk got together and formed a band. For the last few months, they've been riding around, stealing and killing. They're setting up shop in big cities and small ones. It's so bad I heard they might be building a wall."

Lou's dad struggled against the sag in the cushion, but he managed to lean forward. Lou could sense the bewilderment in his voice. "A wall?"

"Yeah," said the woman. "A wall. Either the Cartel wants to keep us in, or the government wants to keep them out. Either way, I hear there's about to be a wall that keeps Texas from the rest of the country. If you ask me, it's how it always should have been. We've always been our own country, am I right?"

The woman cackled and maintained the rhythm of her rocking. With the shotgun still on her lap, she reached across her body and picked up a plastic sports bottle, drew the bottle to her mouth, popped open the sippy top with her dentures, and then squeezed a healthy chug of water into her mouth. She held it in her cheeks, swishing it around, and then swallowed with an audible, childlike gulp.

"River water ain't the best," she said with a drawl that sounded more pronounced the more she spoke. "But it keeps me from keeling over. It is what it is. Am I right?"

Lou ran her tongue along her dry lower lip, dragging it slowly across the cracks that bled if she stretched her mouth too wide. Mild dehydration was a constant since they'd left home. Her dad was good at finding rivers, lakes, and ponds for drinking and bathing, but it wasn't enough.

"How do you know so much about the wall and the…"

"Cartel?"

"Yeah. The Cartel."

The woman looked down at her left hand and rubbed her arthritically swollen thumb across her bare ring finger. "I had a husband. We had two boys."

Lou scanned the room but saw no sign of anyone living in the mobile home. Even the picture frames on the paneled walls were absent of family. They were watercolor drawings of flowers and sloping hills.

"Where are they?" asked Lou.

"The boys," the old woman said, a mournful tone entering her warbling cadence, "they left to get theirs. They joined up with some man named Roof. He was a big shot or something, and they figured it better to be on the porch with the big dogs than in the yard going hungry."

"They joined the Cartel?" asked Lou's dad.

The woman's glare had glazed over. Now she was somewhere else, staring into a past she'd likely just as soon forget. She absently squeezed the bottle in her lap, and water trickled down its side.

"Ma'am?"

Her eyes fluttered and she smacked her mouth. "Yeah," she said. "That they did. We were only a few months after the Scourge. My husband died from the sickness, you know. A lot of people died from the sickness."

"My mom died," said Lou. "So, did my brother."

The woman eyed Lou and frowned. "Sad, ain't it? So many people killed by some little bug ain't nobody could see? And all 'cause of them refugee camps overseas. You know that's where they say it started. Them camps after the war in Syria."

Lou looked at her dad. "What camps?"

"You know," said the woman, "after the war in Syria, all them Syrians left. They went to other places that didn't want them. They built camps. Lots of people in not a lot of space. Some got sick, and it spread like wildfire."

Lou's father put his hand on her leg. "There were other camps too in Eastern Europe. Those are the places the Scourge started. Then it spread."

"I'm sorry your husband died," said Lou.

The woman's face flushed and she smiled. Her eyes squeezed shut, and the crow's-feet that framed them deepened. She took another swig of water.

Lou's dad shifted his weight in the seat and waited for her to finish her drink. "What about your sons?"

"They got crossways with that Roof fella somehow. Roof sent some dog-ugly man named Queho to tell me my boys was dead. He told me matter-of-fact-like that he'd been the one to kill them."

Lou inched next to her father as if she couldn't get close enough. He put his arm around her.

The woman rubbed the shotgun in her lap. "Gave me this here shotgun. Belonged to my older boy."

"He gave you a weapon after telling you he killed your children?" asked Lou's dad.

The woman chuckled, her lips thinning behind the dull veneer of her Chiclets. "That's a thing, ain't it? Told me the gun, which I guess all of them grunts use, was a reminder for me not to mess with the Cartel."

"Grunts?"

"Yeah," she said, stroking the shotgun. "They call 'em grunts, the ones at the bottom of the heap, the little dogs trying to get their nibble on the porch."

"I'm sorry," said Lou's dad. "It's an awful thing to lose a child."

The woman smacked her dentures. "That Queho fella was an ugly one. Did I say that? Mean as a snake. Had a limp as nasty as his breath. I can still smell his breath. It was like sour mash and shellfish."

Lou wrinkled her nose at the vivid description. She pictured Queho in her mind as the kind of desperado she'd read about in her father's Louis L'Amour westerns.

"He was as dark as the two of you," said the woman, motioning with her pointed chin. "No offense or nothing. But I'm guessing he was south of here. You know, one of them illegals."

Lou's father bristled and his glare hardened. "We're not illegals. My father and *his* father were born here. Lou's mother was half Cherokee and half Algerian."

The woman puckered her lips so that they almost closed around her teeth, deepening the tributaries of creases that traveled her face. She pumped her feet to keep the chair rocking. It sounded to Lou like the chair was mocking them with its incessant creak.

"Algerian, you say?" said the woman. "And Cherokee. I'm pure Texan myself. Had an uncle die in the Alamo. Had another killed at Goliad. A third was there when Santa Ana surrendered at San Jacinto. I mean to say they're distant uncles, but kin nonetheless. What are you, Dave?"

"American."

She shook her head. "No. What was your great-granddaddy? What was he? Mexican? Cuban? Puerto—"

"Venezuelan."

"Ah," said the woman. "Venezuelan. So that makes your girl here a pretty little melting pot. You best be careful with your melting pot. Them knives might not be big enough."

Lou watched the vein in her father's neck strain against his reddening skin, the muscles in his forearms tense. His jaw clenched.

Lou thought steam might rise from his head and pour from his nostrils. However, he remained quiet and listened to the woman spin her tales and spout her poison.

The rocking chair creaked, the rhythm unchanged. "That Cartel runs drugs and women," she said. "They're staking claim to everything from El Paso to Orange and Wichita Falls to Corpus. Big cities, small towns, and everything in between."

"That so?" Lou's dad remarked.

She could tell he wasn't really listening to the woman anymore. He was busy planning their exit. She could see it in his eyes, the way he'd inched forward and was perched at the edge of the love seat, ready to stand.

"Sure is," said the woman. "Wherever it is you're going, you won't get there without having to go around them or through them."

Lou's father pressed himself to his feet. "All right. We appreciate all of your help, but we best be going."

The woman stopped rocking.

"So soon?" she asked, her brow knitted more tightly than the throw on the love seat. "That's disappointing. We were just getting to know one another."

Lou's dad faked a smile and touched Lou on the shoulder. "It was a nice visit," he said in a tone Lou knew he reserved for pleasant, shallow conversation, "but we do need to head out. We want to make camp before sundown."

The woman frowned and used the shotgun for leverage to push herself to her feet. Then she held it in both hands and led the pair to her door. Lou sucked in a deep breath of cool air as she exited the trailer and descended the concrete steps to the ground.

As they walked away, the woman called from the doorway. "I don't get too many visitors. I mean, aside from the ugly dog Queho. He comes around every now and then. Where was it you said you were heading?"

Lou's father stopped. He stood with his back to the woman for a moment before looking over his shoulder. "I didn't," he told her.

"So where is it, then?" the woman pressed.

"East," he said. "We're headed east, possibly to Waco."

"All right then. You watch out for that little melting pot of yours. She's gold."

Lou followed her father back to the bench, where he picked up his pack. Hers was still on her back, the padded straps providing little relief from its weight on her shoulders. He slung his pack onto his back and snapped the chest strap shut. He was otherwise quiet and serious, his movements sharp and quick.

"Why aren't we staying here?" she asked. "I thought we were staying here."

"Not now. We need to go."

Lou started to question him, but thought better of it, following him stride for stride back to the highway and across the bridge. The sun had dipped below the horizon, and only the ambient glow of its sinking light was evident to the west.

"It's getting dark," she said when they'd crossed the bridge onto the northern bank of the Colorado River. "We—"

"Just keep up," he cut in between heavy breaths. "I'll explain later."

Lou quickened her pace. Her aching legs struggled to keep up with her father's purposeful strides. The pack bounced on her back, irritating the sore spots on her shoulders. She tucked the knife back into her waistband and slid her thumbs underneath the pack straps. She tightened her grip and tugged down on the straps to lessen the burden.

"I didn't think we traveled at night," she huffed.

"We don't."

"Then why—"

He stopped suddenly and turned to her. "Not now, Lou," he snapped. "I'll explain later. We cannot stay here."

Lou's eyes glistened with the tears she was trying to suppress. A rare combination of exhaustion, fear, and childlike confusion forced the lump back into her throat. She swallowed past it and hurried to stay alongside her father.

They hiked north and west along Farm to Market Road 1431 for more than three hours, Lou's father ignoring her pleas to stop and rest. Occasionally he'd slow and offer her water from his canteen. As soon as she'd slugged enough to keep her hydrated in the dry, cold night air, he'd pick up speed, lunging with each step. Lou was certain he was punishing her for something she hadn't done.

Finally, as it neared midnight, they turned off the main road and cut across a narrow street to one that ran parallel to the eastern bank of the river. Her father slowed when they reached a row of single-story waterfront homes. None of them showed any signs of life: no candlelight flickering through the windows, no smoke or smell of cooked food.

Lou's legs were weak, her back and shoulders hurt, and she had the beginnings of a headache at her temples. Her father walked ahead of her to check one of the houses for inhabitants.

He disappeared around the back of one property, and Lou traipsed into the long driveway to a basketball hoop cemented into the ground to one side. She leaned against the ten-foot pole that braced the basket and waited. The pole was colder than the air and felt good against the side of her head.

She closed her eyes and was almost asleep standing up when her father emerged from behind the house. He hustled to her and calmly instructed her to follow him.

Lou reluctantly let go of the pole and, weak kneed, forced herself to trudge up the driveway and then cut around the right side of the house. There was no garage; the driveway ended at an extension of the one-story house. There was a pair of French doors next to a large bay window. Lou couldn't see through the glass as she passed them, but it looked like that part of the house was a conversion or an addition. It didn't seem right to her that the driveway would end at the front of the house.

"C'mon," said David. "I found a way into the house."

Lou followed him into the knee-high weeds that separated the house from its neighboring property, a similar-sized single-story house. She turned the corner to see a small boat slip at the river's edge. A thin ribbon of moonlight reflected off the dark, wide ripples of the water.

She turned from the water to her father, who was standing against the back of the house. He waved her toward him, and she marched the final few steps, leaned against the painted brick exterior, and adjusted the ball cap on her head.

"This window's open," said her father. "It's a crack, but it's enough."

He pushed his fingers to the single pane and pushed upward with a grunt. The window finished its slide upward, and there was enough room to fit through the opening.

"You first, Lou. You've been a trooper."

Lou mumbled under her breath something a child shouldn't ever say to a parent. Even with the pack on her back, she fit through the open window and crawled onto the cold tile floor of a living room larger than the one they had in Austin.

She moved far enough away from the window to give her father room to climb into the house. He tossed his pack through first, which Lou dragged toward her by the strap, and awkwardly contorted his body through the window and into the house.

Once inside, he gripped the ledge and pulled downward, closing the window and locking it. He exhaled loudly and plopped onto the floor next to Lou.

"Why did we do that?" she asked, barely able to form the words. "I'm only eight. You nearly killed me."

Lou's dad sighed. "I didn't kill you, Lou."

"I said nearly."

"Okay. I didn't *nearly* kill you. But we couldn't stay anywhere near that woman or the town center. We needed to get as far away as we could. We'll keep moving in the morning. Or maybe in the afternoon. I'm as tired as you are."

He stood and walked over to one of two sofas in the middle of the room. It was dark, but Lou could make out the shapes of things.

"You're not as tired as me," she said. "My legs are small. I walked twice as far as you. You nearly killed me."

"You'd be closer to dying if we stayed there, Lou." Her father eased himself onto the sofa. "That woman was warning us."

Lou took off her pack, leaving it on the floor, and slinked over to the other sofa, feeling her way so as not to bump into anything she couldn't see. She found the sofa and climbed onto it like a bed. Her headache was getting worse.

"What?"

"She was warning us. All the talk of the Cartel, how they take things, how you'd be a prize to them. She was telling us to leave without giving it away."

"Why wouldn't she just say it?" said Lou, pulling a pillow from the back of the sofa and placing it under her head.

"I don't know. Maybe it was plausible deniability."

"I don't—"

"Sorry. Plausible deniability is when someone can deny knowing or saying something if they intentionally choose not to know it or say it."

"Oh."

"You did a good job, Lou." Her father nodded. "I know tonight was tough."

"Everything is tough," she said.

"True, but this whole Cartel info changes things for us. It's not about finding food, water, shelter, and staying away from the occasional violence anymore. Now we have to worry about a big gang of people who want to turn Texas into a lawless no-man's-land."

"Are you scared?" Lou asked.

"I've never lied to you. Perhaps I shouldn't be as honest as I am. I know you're a little girl, but I think it's better to talk about reality. That way you're prepared. I'd rather you be alive and frightened than the alternative."

"I'm not frightened," she said. "But my head hurts."

"You're probably dehydrated."

Her father eased next to her and handed her his canteen. Then he held a chalky tablet to her mouth. She recognized it as aspirin and swallowed it with the next swig of water.

He knelt beside her and put his cold hand on her head. Lou sank into the sofa as he explained why they had to leave Marble Falls as fast as they did, and why he wanted to go north and not the direction he'd told the old woman in the trailer.

She closed her eyes and listened to her father talk. It was like he was reading her a fanciful story about bad men in the Wild West. There were gunfights and scared townsfolk. But there was no talk of a hero or of salvation. This was a story for which the ending hadn't been written. She fell asleep, against the throb in her temples, to her father talking about finding the wall and crossing it.

CHAPTER 9

OCTOBER 11, 2033, 10:00 AM
SCOURGE +1 YEAR, 3 DAYS
MARBLE FALLS, TEXAS

Lou's headache was gone when she awoke. She blinked her eyes open, picked the sleep from the corners, rolled the crust around in her fingers, and flicked it onto the floor.

She yawned and stretched her sore back and shoulders, arching on the sofa like a cat. Her tongue was thick, and her mouth felt like it was full of cotton.

The light coming in through the window and glass door on the back of the house told her it was mid-morning. It was bright and without the beautiful warm glow of a sunrise.

She rolled onto her side and stared out the back of the house. Everything looked different in the daylight. The boat slip she'd seen only as a shadowy frame against the flicker of moonlight on the water was actually a trio of finger docks that created a pair of slips. Covering the slips was a red metal slatted roof.

The slip held a pair of watercraft, though from her vantage point, she couldn't tell much about them or how big they might be. The river itself was choppy with a healthy current running south.

Beyond the river, on the opposite bank, the trees were swaying.

The evergreens waved their needles, and what was left of the deciduous leaves flapped and fluttered in the healthy breeze.

Lou's eyes drifted from the windows to inside the house. The sofa where her father had slept was empty.

"Dad?" she called out to him, her voice raspy. She cleared her throat and called him again. "Dad, are you here?"

He appeared from behind a wall beyond the sofa. "You're finally up? Good. Breakfast is served."

He waved at her with a broad smile on his face and disappeared behind the wall. He was whistling an unfamiliar tune, but he sounded happy.

Lou leaned over and plucked her Astros ball cap from the floor and pulled it onto her head. She spun her legs to the floor and gingerly walked to where her father was standing. Her legs reminded her with every step of the arduous trek the day before.

Lou rounded the wall to find herself in a gleaming kitchen of white and silver. Though dusty, the counters were bright white slabs of sharply hewn stone. The appliances were stainless steel, the cabinets a reflective gray laminate, and the floors white pine.

It was a room cut straight from the future, and best of all was what her father was preparing. He was at the counter next to the stove, cranking a manual can opener across the top of a green can. Next to him were some cans, their lids pried open, and bowls filled with bright-colored fruits.

"Are those peaches?" asked Lou, the ache in her legs suddenly absent. "And pears?"

"Yep. There was a nice stack of these in the cupboard. And luckily a can opener."

He shook the black-handled opener in his hand. There was an excitement in his voice Lou hadn't heard in a long time. She stood next to him as he pried back the steel can lid and poured a bowl full of syrupy peaches. He pushed the bowl toward Lou and then stuck a spoon into the bounty.

"Try these first," he said. "Then have the pears. There's also a fruit medley. It has cherries in it."

"I love fruit cups."

He rubbed the cap on her head. "I know. Save it for dessert."

Lou cupped the bowl with both hands and picked it up. "Thank you."

"You're welcome."

Lou carried the bowl from the kitchen to the living room where she'd slept. She set the bowl on a coffee table in front of her on the sofa and then sat on the floor. She crossed her legs, feeling her tight thigh muscles stretch.

She leaned over and inhaled the sugary aroma of the canned peaches. It brought with it memories of her mother in the kitchen, pulling peaches and strawberries from the backyard. The peach trees, along with a lime tree, were in large pots on the back porch. The strawberry plants grew in the tidy garden her mom kept in the back corner of the yard nearest the fence with their neighbors.

The berries ripened earlier than the peaches, but from April through mid-July, her mother was busy with canning and pie baking. She had a green thumb, her dad used to say proudly, and a knack for cooking.

Her peach cobbler with a scoop of home-churned vanilla ice cream was the best. Lou remembered it as fondly as catching fireflies in jars and roasting marshmallows over the fire pit her father had built, with a little help from her brother.

Their life had been idyllic, Rockwellian almost. *Had* been.

Lou closed her eyes and savored the syrupy scent of the peaches. She was sure that was what had her father smiling: the bittersweet memory of their family as it used to be.

Lou scooped the spoon deep into the ceramic bowl, drawing up a full, sloppy slice of fruit. She held it there for a moment and then shoveled it between her teeth. The strong flavor flooded her mouth, and she anxiously devoured the peach, almost forgetting to chew it.

Within minutes she'd devoured the fruit and was holding the bowl to her face, draining what was left of the syrup, when her father walked in with a bowl of pears. He set it on the table in front of her.

"Don't eat too fast," he said. "I don't want you getting sick. I'm not sure if the plumbing works here or not."

Lou licked her lips and started on the pears. She was ravenous, as if the taste of food had triggered a Pavlovian response in her brain.

Her father pulled a folded map from his back pocket, unfolded it, and spread it out on the table. He knelt in front of it and flattened it with his hands. It was worn with rolled corners and hairline tears along the folds. Even in its sorry shape, Lou could tell it was a map of Texas. The map was upside down to her father. He had it facing Lou. She pointed at it with her spoon.

"Where'd you get that?"

"I've had it awhile," he replied. "I look at it occasionally to remind myself of where things are. No GPS now, you know, so we've gotta go old school."

Lou had a pear stored in one cheek. "Global positioning satellite?"

"Yes," her father said approvingly. "Good memory, Lou. You're a smart one. Did I ever tell you that you were reciting poetry at fifteen months old?"

"Yes. Robert Frost."

One corner of his mouth curled into a smile. "That's right. Now let's see if you can memorize key parts of this map."

Lou's father ran his finger across the crinkled paper. He showed her major highways and the lesser-traveled farm-to-market roads that intersected or ran parallel to the busier thoroughfares. He showed her where the major cities were, estimated the number of days it would take to walk from one to another, and highlighted the routes that kept her closest to water.

Lou didn't ask questions. She chewed slowly on the pears, absorbing both their flavor and her father's lesson. Her eyes danced from one spot on the map to the next. She pointed to the spot on the

Colorado River where they'd spent the night.

"How did you pick here?" she asked.

"I vaguely remembered seeing a group of homes along the river," he said, his finger tracing the meandering light blue line that represented the Colorado River. "I knew it was northwest of town, I just wasn't sure how far it was. We got lucky."

Lou stopped chewing the last pear. "So, are we staying here? Is this our new home?"

Her father sat back on his heels and sighed, scratched his head, and looked over his shoulder toward the water before frowning. "I don't think so. We can stay here a couple of days, but I don't think we should stay in a house."

Lou dropped the spoon into the bowl with a clang. She sat back on the sofa and folded her arms across her chest. She wasn't pouting, she was considering what her father meant.

"Where will we live if we can't stay in a house?"

He scratched his chin and leaned forward again, rested his elbows on the table, and looked down at the map. He studied the intersecting web of lines and colors that approximated hills and waterways, towns and cities, highways and dirt roads.

"Dad?" Lou pressed.

He held up a finger before lowering it to the map. He tapped the paper. "Here," he said. "I think we go here."

Lou unfolded her arms and scooted to the edge of the sofa, working hard not to sink into the worn foam cushion. She focused on the map at the spot where her father held his finger. It wasn't in Texas.

"Lawton, Oklahoma?"

Her father nodded. "North of the wall before they build it," he said. "If that woman was telling us the truth, the Cartel is only in Texas."

"Oklahoma?"

"I know," he said. "It's not close. It's a good three hundred miles.

That could take us a week. But it'll be worth it."

Lou adjusted the cap on her head, pushing the brim up so she could clearly look at her father. She studied his face. He looked older than he had the day before. His complexion was more ashen, his gray stubble thicker. The dark semicircles under his eyes were blacker than purple, and the lines that ran across his forehead when he questioned something or got angry seemed more permanently etched.

"What if there is a Cartel in Oklahoma?" she asked.

He glanced at his finger on the map and back to Lou. "There could be."

"What if there's no Cartel in Texas?"

He swallowed. "There might not be."

Lou looked past her father, out the window, and to the river. The river sparkled, reflecting the sunlight like facets on a diamond.

"How much more food is in the kitchen?" she asked, her eyes still transfixed by the water.

"A few days' worth if we ration it."

Lou nodded. "I bet there are fish in the river."

Her dad pivoted to follow Lou's gaze. "Probably bass. Catfish. Crappie."

"Catfish is crappy?"

He chuckled. "No, crappie is a fish. And it's pronounced crop-ee. Not bad eating either."

Lou absently stuck her finger into the empty peach bowl and dragged it along the bottom. Then she stuck it into her mouth and sucked off the sweet liquid. Her dad smiled and copied her. He smacked his lips.

"Reminds me of Mom," he said wistfully.

"We can stay here?" she asked.

He sighed. "For now. But at the first sign of trouble, we head north. Deal?"

"Deal."

CHAPTER 10

OCTOBER 31, 2034, 7:14 AM
SCOURGE +2 YEARS, 23 DAYS
MARBLE FALLS, TEXAS

Lou felt a tug on her line. She jerked back the rod, lowered it, and turned the reel handle toward her in a slow counterclockwise motion. The reel spun and the line tugged, drawing more distance between her and whatever fish had taken the bait. She was seated in the front bench of a wide canoe with her feet pressed against both sides of the hull. Her father was behind her, his line slack.

"You got something?" he whispered.

"Yep," said Lou. "It's big, I think, and it's running."

"Good. At least one of us is having luck."

There was a mist hanging over the river at what was the coldest part of the morning. It swirled and danced atop the water, hiding the fishing lines as they dipped underneath the surface. Lou imagined this was what Loch Ness was like. Her father had told her about the legend of the prehistoric monster that dwelled in the Scottish lake.

For a flash, Lou imagined she had the monster on the other end of her line, pawing its way above the riverbed, its webbed claws catching the water to propel it forward. Its scaly underbelly dusted the floor, pushing up clouds of silt as it swam farther away from the canoe and the girl who would eventually reel it in. Like so much in her life these days, reality was mixed with escapist fantasy. Without fantasy, the ten-year-old might not have been able to cope with the grim future she knew, in the dark recesses her young, advanced mind, reality awaited her sooner than later. Even an imaginary confrontation with an aquatic dinosaur was better than the stark days and weeks ahead.

As much as she tried, Lou couldn't focus on the present. She couldn't enjoy the brief respite she and her father had enjoyed the past few weeks. There was no "in the moment" for Lou. She was always looking forward, trying to anticipate what was coming next. She was so preoccupied with the future, she had trouble living in the present.

In a world where there was no foreseeable, acceptable future, that was tormenting. Ignorance would have been bliss. Instead, the brilliant elementary-age child with a gift for memory and for violence chose to escape into fantasy; whether it be in her head, from the stories her father told her, or the pages of a book, Lou relished the parts of her life that weren't real. She sighed and listened to the faint whir and buzz of the reel as the monster on the other end of it fought for its life. Her eyes drifted up from the mist toward the clear predawn sky. The stars twinkled and strobed. Some were still as bright as they'd been all night. Others appeared to be flickering as would a candle about to run out of wick. It was a clear sky. There were no clouds to trap the radiating heat from the earth, so the cold, especially on the water in a canoe, seeped through her clothing. Chill bumps populated her skin. The hair on her neck stood on end. A chill ran through her body and she involuntarily shuddered, holding tight onto the pole.

The sun wouldn't peek above the horizon for another half hour, and there was more than a bite to the late fall air. The canoe was anchored to the silty bottom of the river about two hundred yards downriver from the house.

They'd found it to be a good spot, where the current slowed before rounding a bend and picking up speed. There was an outcrop of smooth gray rocks, covered in a sheen of green moss, that ran from one bank to the middle of the river. It gurgled and babbled as the running water ran over and around the stones. They'd caught a wide variety of fish in the past three weeks. This morning they were hunting bass, having grown tired of catfish and the relatively small size of the black crappie they'd eaten in abundance.

The canoe was fiberglass and wide enough to keep steady during a fight with a strong fish. Lou pulled back on her rod, the tip of it bending against the tug of the fish on the other end of the line.

"Let it run a bit," said David. "He's not got too far to go. He'll get tired fast."

He was right. Within a couple of minutes, Lou was hauling in a large bass. It flopped on the line until she dropped it to the floor of the canoe. Her father picked up the fish and held it for Lou while she worked the hook from its mouth.

Lou had gotten proficient at removing the hooks. At first, she'd been squeamish about the effort. She'd been afraid to hurt the fish. The blood didn't help make her father's case that the fish couldn't feel anything. Lou wondered if what he was saying was true or if he was merely telling her that to get her over the fear of inducing pain. Ultimately, she reasoned it didn't matter. She'd be eating the fish soon enough anyhow.

Once she'd freed the fish, her father dumped it into a Styrofoam cooler they'd found in the backyard of a neighboring house. The cooler was half filled with river water to keep their catch alive until it was time to filet and cook it.

"How many is that now?" she asked, checking her jerk bait to make sure all of the hooks were good and the knot at the end of the line was taut.

Her dad peeked back into the cooler. "Three."

"Let's get another one before we go in. That's two for you and two for me."

"Okay." Her dad chuckled. "One more, Captain Ahab."

Lou tossed her line back into the water near the bank. She kept the line slack and tugged on it a couple of times before letting the bait sit. Then she tugged twice more. The cadence had been working for her all morning.

"Ahab?"

"He's the protagonist in *Moby-Dick*," said her father. He tugged on his line and let the bait drop. "The book is about a whale and a man's obsession with finding it."

"Why does he want to find the whale?"

"The whale bit off his leg. He believes the whale, Moby Dick, is his nemesis. He's consumed with revenge."

Lou tugged twice on her slack line. "Does he find it?"

"Do you want me to ruin the story by telling you?"

Lou looked over at her father. "I don't think I'll ever read it."

"You never know."

"C'mon, tell me."

"I'll say this to you, Lou," he said, plucking the line back to move the bait, "a man consumed with revenge never gets what he wants, does he?"

Lou blinked, considering what her father was saying. She shrugged.

He shook his head. "No. Revenge doesn't digest well. It sticks in your gut, whether you're seeking it or you've achieved it. It's all-consuming one way or the other."

"He doesn't kill the whale?"

"You'll have to read the book. It's—"

His eyes widened and he sat up straight, tightening his grip around the fishing pole. The tip of the pole bent, snapped straight, and then bent again. He pulled on the pole to set the hook and then cranked the wheel.

"Got one," he said, letting the fish run for a moment. "It's about time."

"You're not kidding." Lou grinned. "You'd starve without me."

Her father smirked and worked the fish back toward the canoe. As he'd taught Lou to do, he braced his feet against the outer edges of the hull to keep from rocking the canoe too much as he wound the line shorter. The fish had about given up its fight when Lou called out to her father. He ignored her.

"Dad," she stressed, "turn around."

The frustration on his face melted into concern once he listened to her and looked over his shoulder and back toward the home in which they'd been squatting for the past three weeks. There was a tall, thin man on the shore, and he was holding the Mossberg as if it were his own. Behind him was a squatty woman, who was half his height but broad shouldered. Her fisted hands were planted forcefully on her hips.

From the distance, Lou couldn't see the expressions on their faces. That was irrelevant and there wasn't enough sunlight yet. Even in the gray light of the predawn, their body language said everything she needed to know.

"I think this is their canoe," said Lou.

Lou's father drew the pole into the hull and shifted his weight to better watch the people on the bank. He glanced at Lou and back at them. Then he raised his arm and waved at them as if they were lifelong friends. When he spoke to her, he kept a broad smile on his face. His voice reminded Lou of the amateur ventriloquist who'd visited her school a couple of times.

"I think that's their house too," he said.

Lou mimicked her father. She smiled broadly and raised a hand high into the air to wave hello. "That's your gun though."

"Yep," he said through his teeth. "Should have brought it with me. Never thought I'd need a rifle for fishing."

"I have my knives. Both of them."

The smile evaporated from his face and he glared at her. "Don't even think about it. They're not going to hurt us."

"How do you know?"

"Trust me."

He dropped the pole entirely and waved both hands over his head in surrender before he cupped them around his mouth. "We're unarmed," he called. "I'm with my ten-year-old daughter. We're coming back."

The man and woman exchanged glances, seemed to say something to one another, and the man lowered the rifle from his shoulder. He did, however, keep it pointed in their general direction.

"You best hurry up," said the man, the breeze carrying his voice over the rush of the water.

Lou's father picked up his rod and reel and cranked in the line. He swung the dangling fish, another bass, over toward Lou, and she pulled out the hooks. Two of the four-pronged twines had set deep into the fish's mouth. Its wide, glassy eyes stared back at her as she freed it from the barbs and tossed it into the cooler.

She drew in her line, and the two of them dropped their poles into the bottom of the canoe. He slowly pulled up the anchor from the riverbed and set it next to the cooler.

The canoe started moving with the current, away from the angry couple on the bank. Lou's dad picked up the lone paddle he'd brought with them and started pulling it through the water. He worked it to one side to turn the canoe against the slow-moving current, and then switched to the other side of the canoe. He dug deep into the river, drawing two strokes with the paddle before alternating.

The canoe lurched underneath them with each long pull and then drifted askance until Lou's father had drawn another pull against the water. He was huffing and a thin sheen of perspiration had bloomed on his forehead by the time they'd made it to the bank a few yards from the couple.

The man again drew the rifle to his shoulder, keeping it aimed at Lou's father as Lou hopped out of the canoe onto the bank and helped tug it halfway onto the land. Lou's father lowered the paddle and used the sides of the canoe to balance himself as he exited.

Once on land, he raised his hands above his head and told Lou to do the same. They stood still, not approaching the couple.

"Who are you?" barked the man. His voice was deep and resonant and carried the Texas twang most people from the state couldn't even hear. It was too familiar.

"My name is Dave. This is my daughter, Lou. We're from Austin. We've been here a few weeks."

The woman stepped forward, her big feet clomping in the weeds with a crunching sound. She pointed her finger at Lou and then her father. "You been in our house?" she asked with a tone that revealed she knew the answer. "You been eating our food, sleeping in our beds?"

Lou chuckled then immediately silenced the unfortunate giggle by pressing her mouth closed. Her father shot her a glare that somehow conveyed both anger and bewilderment.

The woman scowled, her eyebrows merging into one hairy caterpillar.

"You find that funny, young'un?" she sniped. "You think trespassin' and stealin' from folks is funny?"

Lou, her lips still pressed into a flat line, shook her head. "No."

"Then why, pray tell, were you laughin'?"

Lou checked with her father, who nodded tacit approval, before she answered the woman. She shrugged. "Because you made us sound like Goldilocks. Robert Southey's book about—"

"I know who Goldilocks is," the woman harrumphed. "I never found it funny."

The man holding her father's gun chuckled. The gun quavered with the rise and fall of his body.

The woman snapped her attention toward him. "What?" she said, her ire directed at her man.

"That *was* sorta funny," he said. "I mean, you did say that they—"

She threw back her head in defiance and again planted her fists on her hips. "It's *not* funny, Theodore. These here folks stole from us, and you're gonna laugh at 'em?"

He lowered the rifle. "I'm laughing at you, Earlene," he said. His voice sounded much less barbed with twang when compared to hers. "She's a ten-year-old girl."

The woman frowned and eyed Lou up and down. "She looks like a boy," she said, as if Lou would find that offensive.

"Can we explain?" Lou's father interjected. "I'm not making an excuse here. Under normal circumstances we'd never dream of breaking into someone's home and eating their food. We—"

"For all we know," interrupted the woman, her square jaw flexing, "they got the Scourge. They could be sick. Now they infected everything we got."

"We're not sick," Lou countered.

"We're not," her father confirmed. "We're immune. Like you. And we're just trying to survive. Like you."

The woman's glare softened, if only for a blink, and she stepped back toward the man. He leaned into her and whispered something into her ear. She initially resisted whatever it was he said. But the more he spoke, the more her tension eased. Finally, she nodded.

Still holding the Mossberg in his left hand, the man extended his right. "I'm Teddy Gamble. This here is my wife, Earlene. That's our canoe you been using, and that's our river house you been sleeping in. We just managed to get here from Hallettsville. Got us a ranch there."

Lou's father shook the man's hand. "We'll collect our stuff and be on our way. If you need to keep the Mossberg as payment, I'll—"

"Just managed?" Lou exclaimed. "We've been here a year."

The woman scowled. Lou's father rolled his eyes, letting her know that was information she need not have shared.

The man smiled at Lou while he held his handshake grip tight. "No need to skedaddle just yet." He motioned toward the canoe. "What did you catch?"

"Bass," Lou's dad replied. "Four of them."

"I caught three of them," said Lou.

The man smiled and winked at her. "I bet you did."

He let go of his grip and sucked in a deep breath of the cool dawn air. "Tell you what," he said, "Earlene is a mean cook. She can fry up them fish and we can have a nice meal before you go. Consider that your payment."

Earlene started to protest, but Teddy turned to her and smirked. "Deal?"

She waved her finger at Lou and her father. "Fine," she huffed. "But the two of them need to be gone by sundown. I want my house to myself. We came here for peace and quiet."

She spun on her heavy feet and marched back to the house. Her arms swung at her sides, but her shoulders remained remarkably still. Lou thought she moved like a tank across rough terrain.

Teddy switched the Mossberg to his right hand and started toward the canoe. Unlike his wife, he slinked like a praying mantis. His strides were long and his knees popped from their joints with each step. "Don't mind Earlene," he said. "She's what I like to call passionate. She gets heated in a hurry. She likes to boil instead of simmer."

Lou and her father followed Teddy back to the canoe. When they reached it, Teddy stood on the bank and looked across the water. The mist was lifting.

"Don't get me wrong," he said without turning around. "You *did* break into our river house. You *did* eat our food. It ain't like she's got no reason to be riled up."

Lou's father climbed into the canoe, dragging his hand along one edge to balance himself. He gripped the cooler and picked it up with both hands. The water sloshed around inside it, some of it spilling out one side. Slowly, he wobbled back onto the bank and set down the cooler.

Teddy sighed. "But I understand. In times like these, you gotta do whatchu gotta do."

When he spoke, his long I's sounded more like "ahhh". Every syllable sounded to Lou as if it became two.

Teddy chuckled. "Earlene says I'm too softhearted. Maybe so. Softhearted enough to let you break bread with us and rest up before you go. But not softhearted enough to hand over your rifle just yet."

He drew it up to his shoulder and held it properly, motioning toward the house with the barrel. Lou was confused. On one hand he was holding them at gunpoint. On the other, he was inviting them in to eat a meal.

"I guess I have to share my fish with you?"

"Lou," said her father curtly. Carrying the cooler at his side, it squeezed as he moved.

Teddy smiled widely, revealing a couple of missing teeth. His eyes disappeared when he smiled, and wide crowfeet framed the narrow slits. "Well, I think that's a fair trade. You give us a couple of your hard-earned bass and we let you have the other two. You did catch 'em with my rods and my canoe."

Lou kicked a toe into the weed-ridden dirt and mumbled under her breath. She didn't like the idea of sharing her food even if Teddy had a valid point.

They walked into the house through a back door that led into the kitchen. Earlene had already laid out a cutting board, a rubber mallet, and a filleting knife. There were also a couple of onions and a trio of small potatoes clustered on the counter. She was wearing an apron embroidered with the saying "If you don't kiss the cook, you can kiss my sweet patootie."

Lou smirked at it, not understanding why anyone would buy such a thing. It wasn't funny. Nothing about the couple was funny. This was as much her home now as it was theirs. She'd begun to believe they'd never have to leave. In the year-plus they'd squatted in the house, they hadn't seen a single person until now. It was the perfect hiding place, and it provided for an outstanding training environment.

Every day, her father had led her through exercises, strength training, and flexibility maneuvers. There was weekly gun training, knife throwing, and basic martial arts. She was a wiry little jujitsu warrior. Her biggest downfall was her size. Her hands and arms were too small to effectively operate the Mossberg. Knockout holds were difficult, but her legs were strong enough to do the trick. At least her father told her they would be. He'd never allowed her to knock him unconscious. Now all of it was over.

Lou glared at Earlene, resisting the powerful urge to climb the woman's back, drop her to the floor, and choke her out. She imagined five different ways she could overpower the woman and silently remove her from the equation without making more than a whisper of sound. But Earlene interrupted her fantasy with an order.

"All right then, hand over the fish. I got work to do."

Lou's father set the cooler on the counter next to the cutting board. He opened the top and pulled out a wiggling bass and handed it over to Earlene. She snatched it from him and slapped it onto the cutting board. Holding it with one hand, she picked up the mallet with the other and slammed it on to the bass's head above its eyes. The fish flapped its tail once more and stopped.

Lou stared at the fish and then at the woman. There was something joyful in the way Earlene pounded the life out of the catch. A chill ran down Lou's spine. Maybe the woman would have put up a fight.

Earlene pointed the mallet at her. "You gonna stand there? Or are you and your daddy gonna go clean up my bedroom? I seen you messed it up. No need to wash sheets or nothin'. We gotta save water where we can, and washin' them in the river will just make 'em stiff. Just make the beds nice and neat like. Hospital corners and all."

Lou looked to her father. He motioned toward the family room with his head. As they walked out, Earlene instructed Teddy to go outside and light a fire. She'd be ready soon enough to put on the kettle.

David led Lou into the master bedroom. They'd been sleeping there since their second night in the house. Lou walked to one side of the king-sized mattress. Her father stood on the other.

"I don't like them," Lou said. "The woman is mean, and the man is taking half of our fish."

David took the sheet corner at the foot of the bed and draped it over the edge of the mattress. "We're in their home, Lou," he said softly. "He could have shot us on sight."

"We had no way of knowing if anyone would ever come back. Plus, I don't like how she talks to you."

Lou grabbed her corner at the foot of the bed and tried to match what her father had done. Together they slid to the middle of the bed and evened the sheet.

"How do you think your mother would have reacted, Lou? If somebody had snuck into our house when we weren't there, ate our food, pretended like the place was theirs?"

Lou smirked and moved to the headboard. She folded over the sheet at the top and flattened it with her palm.

"Lou," her father repeated, "what do you think your mother would have done?"

"She'd have shot them on sight," Lou conceded.

"Exactly."

Lou moved to the foot of the bed and, without the two of them saying anything to one another, they simultaneously picked up the crumpled blanket, shook it out, and laid it neatly atop the sheet. They moved as if mirror images of one another.

"Still," she said, "I don't like them."

"You don't like that we have to leave. You like it here."

Lou dropped to her knees to tuck the blanket edge under the

mattress and exhaled audibly. She didn't disagree, which was saying something.

Her dad was bent at his waist, tucking in his side of the blanket. Lou knew he was watching her. She didn't want to look at him. Doing so would only acknowledge he was right.

"Look," he said, edging around the foot of the bed to meet her on her side, "we'll be fine. Let's use this meal to learn a little bit more about what's out there. They may be able to help us avoid making mistakes."

Lou spun the Astros cap around on her head and pulled the bill down over her face. She made sure her light sweatshirt was untucked and bloused so her hosts couldn't see the blades she had tucked against her hips.

Her father put his hand on her shoulder, gently guiding her back to the family room. As they moved, he bent over and whispered, "Keep the knives where they are. We're not going to need them."

Lou rolled her eyes. She wasn't convinced. "Fine."

***

If Lou had felt like giving a compliment, which she didn't, she would have kissed the cook. The bass, three-quarters of which she'd caught, was as delicious as anything she'd had since the Scourge. It wasn't canned peaches, but it was close. She dragged her finger along her empty plate and stuck it into her mouth, sucking on it. Earlene shot her a disapproving look that almost hid the hint of an appreciative smile.

"The flavor is wonderful," her father said. "Thank you."

"You're welcome," Earlene said begrudgingly. "It's the onions."

It was late morning, close to eleven o'clock, Lou guessed by the sun, and they were sitting at a picnic table in the backyard. Ordinarily it would have been too cold to eat outside. But Earlene had refused to serve lunch in her dining room.

"It's reserved for *invited* guests," she'd insisted to her husband. He'd acquiesced and set the tinfoil-covered plate of fish on the outdoor table next to a pot of boiled potatoes.

Having finished her meal, Lou ran her fingers along the peeling burgundy paint on the wood picnic table. It was rough under her touch, and flecks cracked off as she rubbed against them. The conversation had been sparse while the foursome ate. Now that the meal was ending, the talking began in earnest.

"Tell me more about your wife and son," said Earlene, dangling a fork in her hand. She licked her teeth and smacked her lips. "They died?"

"Yes," said Lou's father. "Our son, Davey, got sick first. Then my wife contracted it. It didn't take long before they were both gone."

"Where'd you bury them?" asked Earlene, her expression unchanged.

Lou bristled. She wanted to pull out a knife and hurl it straight between her beady eyes. That, she was sure, would erase the smug, dispassionate expression from the linebacker's face. She picked at the paint with her thumb and let her father handle Earlene with adult diplomacy.

"We didn't," said her father. "We burned them. We lived in a neighborhood. The lots were small. There were a lot of nearby homes. I worried about—"

"You don't have to explain it to us," said Teddy. "What you did makes perfect sense. No judgment from us. We know what you been through, sure enough. We lost—"

"That's none of their business," interrupted Earlene. "They're not invited guests. They're intruders, far as I'm concerned. They ain't got no need to know nothin' about us."

A sadness washed across Teddy's face and his shoulders slumped. He dragged his fork across his plate, pushing around what was left of the potato.

"I'm sorry," said David.

Earlene took a sip of water from her cup and swallowed audibly. She plopped the cup onto the table and sneered. "For what?"

"Your loss. Whoever it was, however many it was, I'm sorry."

Earlene's stone facade cracked for a split second. A glint of pain flashed in her eyes and her posture softened. Then she steeled herself and cleared her throat. "But you're not sorry for breaking into our house?"

"No," Lou answered. "My dad did what he thought he needed to do to keep us safe from the Cartel. He protected me. He's a hero. If you were in the same position, I'd hope you'd do the same for your family. We didn't know anyone would ever be coming—"

Lou's dad put his hand on her back. "Lou," he said gently, "that's enough."

The slightest hint of a smile sparked across Earlene's face. She sat back in her chair and set her fork diagonally across her plate. She picked up a paper napkin and wiped her face so heavy-handedly Lou thought the woman might take off her skin and reveal a serpent underneath. Earlene narrowed her gaze at Lou and then eyed her father.

"How old did you say she is?" she asked.

Lou stared at her. "I'm nine."

"You speak too good for a ten-year-old," said Earlene. "Truth be told, you're a right pipsqueak size-wise. No bigger than a bug. But you talk good. You must be smart."

Lou stopped picking at the table, sat up straight, and pulled her shoulders back. "My dad says I'm incorrigible."

For the first time the woman's features softened and she laughed. She laughed so hard the table shook. Her broad shoulders shuddered and her thick legs bounced against the table legs. "I don't know whether or not to believe a thing ya'll said yet," said Earlene, "but I right as rain believe that."

Lou wasn't sure to be more surprised by the woman's sudden burst of humanity or that she knew the definition of incorrigible.

Either way, she saw an opening.

"He also says the world is made up of two kinds of people," Lou went on. "Those who are smart, and those who think they are."

Earlene slapped her hand on the table so hard Lou jumped in her seat. Earlene pointed her finger at Lou with wide-eyed agreement. "I say the same thing to Theodore. You got your smart folks and your stupid ones who think they got things all figured out."

Lou nodded in agreement while wondering to herself which group Earlene thought she belonged to. She was pretty certain she knew.

"What else does your daddy say?" said Earlene. "You got my interest now."

Lou hesitated and glanced at her father. He gave her a knowing glance that told her it was okay to keep talking, sharing their family wisdom. He must have sensed the same opening.

"He also said the jails were full of stupid people, because if all the crooks were smart, the cops would never catch anybody."

Earlene wagged her finger at Lou and then at her husband. "What I tell you, Theodore? If your cousin Beaufort had a lick of sense in him, he wouldn't have been caught. I told you he was thicker than cement on a hot afternoon."

She looked back at Lou with her hand pulled alongside her mouth. She lowered her voice, to feign keeping a secret from Teddy. "All the stupid comes from his side of the family," she said with a wink.

Teddy rolled his eyes. "I can hear you, Earlene."

All four of them laughed. After a collective sigh, Earlene said, "My own daddy used to call me incorrigible. It was his favorite word for me. Not pretty, not smart, not sweet. Incorrigible. I had no idea what that word meant for years. Finally, I Googled it. I wasn't sure how to take it. But he was my daddy. He had to mean it in a way that told me he loved me."

Her eyes shifted to David and she tilted her head to one side. He smiled at her. She appeared as though she might say something else, but didn't. A brief quiet fell across the table. The chilly breeze, which had whipped up the river, rustled through the trees on the opposite bank. The water lapped at the edge nearest them. Lou looked up toward the sun. It had to be close to noon.

"If we're going to leave," she said to nobody in particular, "we might want to go. We've only got five or six hours of daylight."

The others' eyes followed hers skyward. Earlene squeezed her eyes and shielded them with her hand. The woman was still an assaulting tank, Lou thought, but somehow, she'd retreated during their meal. Lou wondered why a silly mention of a familiar word had struck the woman the way it had and essentially flipped her attitude one hundred and eighty degrees. It didn't make sense.

Nothing in the world made sense anymore. Nothing except her dad's love for her.

"Good idea," said David. He stood, lifting a leg over the bench seat, and picked up his plate. "We'll be heading out now."

"Where will you be going?" asked Teddy.

Lou followed her dad's lead and collected her plate and cutlery. She reached for Earlene's plate, to be polite, but the woman waved her off.

"We're headed east," said David.

"We want to avoid the Cartel," Lou added.

The two of them started toward the entrance that led to the kitchen. Lou balanced a pair of cups on her plate.

Teddy stood, took his wife's plate, and stacked it atop his. "You best be careful, then," he said. "That Cartel is the real deal."

David stopped short of the doorway and looked over his shoulder at Teddy. "You know about them?"

Earlene chuckled and shook her head. Teddy looked at her and then back at David. "They're bad folks," he said. "They're spreading like the Scourge, and they ain't nice about it."

Earlene pushed away from the table and barreled toward the kitchen entrance, rumbling past the others. As she passed them, she grumbled about the Cartel and how they were ruining Texas. "They forced us from our place in Hallettsville," she said. "Wasn't no way for us to stay. They was taking people's land left and right. We got out as quick as we could once we knew we couldn't fight 'em."

"They're as bad as we've heard?" asked David. He stood at the entrance, holding open the door with his foot for Lou and Teddy to walk inside.

"I don't know what you've heard," said Teddy, "but they're bad. They got a headquarters of some sort in Lubbock, and they got people in every city and town. And they're armed."

"Shotguns?" asked David.

"They got some rifles," said Teddy. "We seen 'em. They got trucks and gasoline too. But yeah, most of 'em are carrying shotguns."

Earlene dumped the plates into the sink with a clang. "We heard they broke into some armory or depot of some kind. It was packed with shotguns. They took 'em and handed 'em out."

"I think they like the sound they make when they rack 'em," said Teddy. "They rule with fear, not bullets or shells."

Earlene took the pot of potato water and poured it into the sink. She dipped the plates into it.

"That's not to say they don't use 'em. We seen 'em kill plenty of folks. Stay off the main roads. A lot of 'em are riding horses now. And keep your girl close. Shoot first if it comes to it. Ain't a good one among 'em."

David asked more questions about the strength of the Cartel, the size of their traveling groups, which Teddy called posses, and which roads might be better than others.

At the sink, Earlene scrubbed the plates with the potato water. It sloshed around in the cast-iron basin and splashed onto the countertops.

Lou walked across the kitchen floor, not wanting to listen to the men talk about strategy. She was more interested in the enigma cleaning dishes with dirty water. She sidled up beside Earlene. The woman smelled like a mixture of sweat and strawberry hand soap.

"Can I help?" asked Lou.

Earlene stopped scrubbing and looked down at Lou. She towered over the young girl and, if so inclined, could have squashed her with her meaty thumb and forefinger. The woman sucked in a deep breath and sighed as her eyes welled. Her lower lip quivered. The tank had a weakness.

"You remind me of my girl," she said. "I mean, you're darker than her, of course, but there's something in your eyes. There's a grit there."

Lou stood quietly next to Earlene. She didn't know what to say.

Earlene wiped her eyes with the back of her hands. A trail of bubbles from the soapy potato water hung on her cheek. "That's what made me so mad," she said. "I mean to say you breakin' into my place made me mad. I don't like nobody sleepin' in my bed but me and Theodore. But when I saw your eyes, I got angry."

"Why?"

"The Scourge took her," said Earlene. "She was eighteen. But she was still my baby. She passed in my arms. I was holding her and…"

Earlene stopped. She set her jaw and swallowed. Her temples flexed. Tears streaked down her face.

Lou reached out and, for a reason she didn't understand, she took Earlene's hand and squeezed it. Of course, her hand could only wrap around three of the woman's fingers, but the sentiment was there.

Earlene pulled Lou toward her and enveloped her in a hug that took away Lou's breath. She squeezed and sobbed. Her body shuddered. Lou held onto the woman, a lump forming in her own throat. Her eyes stung with tears.

When they let go of their emotional embrace, Lou saw both of the men staring agape at them. Neither of them seemed to know what to make of it.

"What?" said Earlene, the familiar accusatory growl returning to her voice. She cleared her throat and wiped her eyes. "Can't a girl have a cry?"

Lou adjusted her hat and wiped her face. She stared at the kitchen floor for a moment before looking up to find her father's eyes. They were glistening. He smiled weakly.

Lou exhaled. "We should go," she said, "before it gets too late."

"Before it gets too late," Earlene echoed. "That's a good plan."

The woman tightened the apron at her waist and resumed the task of cleaning the dishes. She sniffed a couple of times but didn't look back at Lou as she and her father walked from the kitchen.

Lou stopped at the doorway to the living room and gripped the door molding. She peeked her head back around the corner toward Earlene. "Thank you," she said. "Everything was just right."

Earlene waved at her without turning around. "You go now."

Lou spun on her boot heel to see Teddy handing the Mossberg back to her dad. David shook Teddy's hand.

"I took the rounds out of the magazine," said Teddy. "It's in your girl's pack. Just a precaution, you know. Can't have too soft a heart."

"Thank you," David said.

The two of them donned their packs, a familiar ache reminding Lou's shoulders of the drudgery to come, and they marched from the house onto the long driveway. The sun was at its peak. They had hours of hiking ahead of them and, for the second time, they had no place to call home.

CHAPTER 11

Lou was out of breath, but she kept running. Her pack slapped against her back and swung from side to side as she skittered across the street to find another hiding place. Her father was a step behind her, urging her to hurry.

She nearly tripped on the curb when she reached the awning-covered sidewalk at City Hall. She banged her knee into an empty planter box and spun to one side before regaining her balance. She limped a couple of steps toward the adjacent building, a place called The Iron Trail, and ducked down behind a large piece of painted plywood nailed vertically between two posts at the building's entrance. It provided a shield of sorts and was a good spot to hide behind.

Her father joined her, squatted, and dropped a knee to the ground. One hand held the Mossberg, and he used the other to balance himself.

"You okay?" he whispered between heaving breaths.

"Fine," said Lou. "I banged my knee, but I'm fine."

He checked his rifle. "I need to reload. Can you keep an eye out?"

"It's hard to see anything. It's too dark."

"Keep an ear out, then. If you hear anything, you let me know."

Lou winced in pain and rubbed her knee. "How many do you think are left?"

"I don't know," her father wheezed. "There were eight of them, I think. I got three or four."

"Will they come after us? Do you—"

"Lou," he snapped, "shush. Listen."

Lou had more questions. She knew her father didn't have the answers, but simply asking them would have made her feel better. It would have made her feel less exposed.

She closed her eyes and listened. Beyond the sound of her father reloading the rifle's magazine, she could hear the crickets chirping in the distance. They'd gone quiet when the gunfire started. Now they were back.

They'd dragged their way into Archer City before the orange sunset had deepened into a siren red. It wasn't on their planned route, but they needed to stay off the highway, as they had for the past nine days. A trip to Oklahoma that should have taken five or six days at most was going to be at least ten. It had to be that way, her dad had explained.

The farther off the beaten path they traveled, the better. He'd done a good job of finding water when they were thirsty and food when they were hungry. Lou had become ridiculously fast at field dressing any mammal or bird they caught. She'd considered hanging pelts and feathers from her belt alongside her knives. Her dad suggested that was too much. No need to advertise, he'd said.

The trek, though slower than they'd hoped, had been relatively uneventful. David had insisted that if they stuck to their plan, fought through the blisters on top of blisters that formed on their insoles and heels, and exhibited patience, they'd never see the Cartel. He'd been right, until twenty minutes ago.

They'd decided to camp in Archer City for the night. It was

approximately on their way north and appeared to be abandoned. They'd walked the perimeter of the town's center, as her dad insisted they do every time they planned to camp in what had once been civilization.

They hadn't seen anyone. It wasn't until they came across the Royal Theater on the corner of Main and Sycamore that they'd found the trouble they'd successfully avoided in the nine days since leaving Marble Falls.

Lou was walking ahead of her father. She was hungry and was hunting for something to eat. Despite complaining to her dad that finding food in a town was harder than in the woods or the overgrown fields that stretched endlessly along both sides of the backroads they traveled, she remained focused on finding something meaty to have for dinner.

Typically, when they were in a town, the menu was limited to rats, mice, and the occasional snake. A lame bird might be a treat. It was always a hard slog to find any of them, given that none of them liked to be around people. However, Lou spotted something more appealing in Archer City, something that would help satiate her hunger.

A stray cat skittered across the street. It was bony. That much she could tell even in the dark. She didn't really want to kill it or eat it. Lou liked cats. Sort of.

In truth, she loved kittens. She vaguely remembered playing with a neighbor's litter after their aging cat had given birth. She'd begged her parents for a kitty. She had gone as far as to pick out her favorite kitten and name it Garfield. But they'd resisted. They got her a goldfish. It had lasted three weeks before it went belly up. That, they'd said, was proof she wasn't old enough to have a pet.

She hustled to follow the cat, knowing it could lead her to other food. Despite its malnourished appearance, it was alive. That meant it was eating something.

With her attention focused on the cat, she wasn't paying diligent attention to her surroundings. Her father hung back, letting her give chase through the weedy alleys between the low-slung buildings that populated the barren downtown streets.

It wasn't until she bumped into the man in the white hat that she saw him. He was tall and lean. His thick beard hid half of his face and the wide brim of the Stetson darkened the other half. His body was all muscle. At least it felt that way when she ran into him.

She stopped cold, bounced off him, and nearly fell to the ground. He reached out and grabbed her arm, holding her for a moment before she shook free.

"Hey," he said gruffly, "where are you headed in such a hurry?"

Lou backed up a step. She glanced past the man, looking for the cat, spotting the shadowy figures of two other people. One of them was wearing a hat.

"You all by yourself?" asked the bearded muscle man. "Little girls shouldn't be traveling by themselves. Bad things could happen."

The man, who she could now see had pistols strapped at his hips, stepped forward. His boots dragged along the crumbs of asphalt that littered the aging alley. The figures behind him drew closer, and two more emerged. At least two of them carried long guns. Lou couldn't tell if the others were armed.

"You deaf?" asked the man. "Dumb?"

Lou backed up a couple of steps, giving herself more distance with long strides, spun, and started to run back to where she'd last seen her father. She was too late.

She didn't make it ten yards before the man caught her. Somehow, the bearded muscle man was incredibly nimble. When he grabbed her, Lou tripped over his boot. Together they tumbled forward and skidded across the alley and out into the street.

The man grabbed her, using his strength and weight advantage to gain leverage. He was telling her to calm down, insisting he wasn't going to hurt her while trying to pin her awkwardly to the ground.

Lou screamed and squirmed. And reached for her knives.

She found one of them with her left hand. She was on her side, and the man was on top of her, lying perpendicular across her body as he worked to maintain control. The ball cap was low over her eyes, blinding her.

She gripped the handle, ignoring his order to calm down, lifted her arm away from her body, and jabbed it at the man. He cried out in pain, cursing loudly, and momentarily lost his hold of her. The blade drove deep into his flesh, and she withdrew it before driving it into the man again. He grunted and spasmed, losing his grip and rolling away from her onto the ground. She pulled free and her hat loosened on her head. For a moment she caught a good look at his face. His teeth dug into his lower lip. His eyes were squeezed shut until he popped them open. His pinprick pupils stared at her, searching for help he knew wouldn't come from her. Lou scrambled to her feet and sprinted away from him.

The other men shouted at her. She ignored them as the crack of gunfire chased her up the street. Lou breathlessly skidded wide around a corner, where she met her father. He was on a knee, his Mossberg pulled tight to his shoulder. Lou slid past him, lost her balance, and stumbled to the ground.

Behind her the gunfire sounded like a cacophony of firecrackers. One pop bled into the next. She pushed herself to her feet, inhaling deeply to catch her breath, the acrid odor of gunpowder filling her nostrils.

Her father was pressed against the side of a single-story building. Lou huddled behind him as he fired one round after another at the approaching threat. Muzzle flashes strobed in the dark, giving away their positions as they fired their weapons.

"Dad," Lou said, "there was a man. He grabbed me. I—"

"Not now," he said, pivoting to fire another volley. "Stay down."

Lou crouched lower to the ground. Her pulse throbbed in her neck. Her heart pounded against her chest. She shifted her weight and balanced herself with her hands. She'd forgotten she still held the one knife in her hand. The blade was stained dark. She dropped it and put her hands up to her ears, pressing her palms flat against the sides of her head. She kept her eyes on the ground, focusing on the blood coating the blade, drowning out the deafening gunfire and the grunts and cries of pain from the targets on the other end of her father's aim. Bullets zipped over her head. The blasts from the shotguns were too far away to reach them.

It wasn't until her father gripped her shoulder, knocking her off balance, that she blinked back to the moment. His face was wrinkled with worry. Even in the dark, she could see the fear in his eyes.

"Run," he ordered her, his words echoing in her mind. They'd sprinted until they found refuge behind the plywood boards. They'd escaped the onslaught until they hadn't.

"I'm reloaded," said David.

Lou nodded. Her eyes were still closed as she strained to hear noises beyond the symphony of insects. She opened them when her father touched her face.

"Are you bleeding? Are you hurt?"

Lou looked at her father's hand. There was blood streaked across his fingers. She instinctively reached up and slid her hand across her face and into her hair, knocking the Astros ball cap askew. Then she remembered the blade.

"No," she said. "It's not my blood."

Her father exhaled as if he'd been holding his breath for too long. His body relaxed. She hadn't even realized how tense he'd been at the thought of her being injured. He started to say something but was interrupted by the zip of a bullet tearing overhead. It crashed into the building behind them, drilling into the masonry.

They turned their attention back to the street.

"I don't see them," Lou whispered.

"Wait," her father said under his breath. He backed off his heels and lay prone on his stomach. He slid the rifle barrel in a gap between the two vertical pieces of painted plywood.

Lou sat down and hugged her knees. Her body was shivering; it wasn't from the cold. All the training and hunting in the world hadn't prepared her for the feel of the steel piercing human skin. She'd felt the sensation of the blade puncturing him and then spreading the wound open. She'd reacted instinctively to the man's attack. She'd stabbed him. Twice.

Now, as the gunfire erupted again, her mind distanced itself from the violence surrounding her. Ten-year-olds never were equipped to see such things, to do such things.

With her arms wrapped around her legs, she opened her palms and looked at her hands. The left one was bloodied. She'd stabbed a man before, in her home. She'd struck bone that time. But for some reason, this was different.

Each time her father pulled the Mossberg's trigger, she felt the vibration of the percussive release of the bullet in her body. One violent throb after another rattled her core.

Lou was absent from the fight. She was stuck in neutral, fixated on the image of the bearded man's face. Was it his face that had her frozen? The feeling of the slicing blade? Or was it the realization that what had happened in their home wasn't a one-off she could file away in the back of her mind and pretend it never happened?

"Lou!" her dad yelled. "I need more ammo."

Lou shook herself into service and found another loaded magazine in the open pack on the cement next to her. She fumbled with it and handed it to her father. The sounds of battle she'd managed to mute exploded into full stereo sound. It sounded as if there were a dozen or more weapons firing at them in a constant barrage of bullets and buckshot.

She slid away from her dad and toward the edge of a plywood board. There were three or four muzzle flashes that burst in succession in front of her. Lou couldn't tell how far away they were, but she couldn't imagine it was more than ten or fifteen yards. That was too close. She slid back behind the plywood and curled into a ball. She was paralyzed.

Her father had reloaded again and begun returning fire. Lou covered her ears with her hands and tried to force the image of the bearded man's face from her mind. Gradually, the sound of gunfire dissipated. Then it stopped and Lou jumped when her father touched her back.

"Lou, we got 'em."

She heard him but didn't understand what he meant. She searched his face as she would a stranger.

He drew closer to her. "Lou, we're okay. They're gone."

Lou nodded but didn't move. "Gone?"

"Gone," he said. "All of them."

"Are you sure?"

"Yes. I'm sure."

He held out his hand and Lou took it so he could pull her up to her feet. When she stood shakily, he wrapped his arms around her and pulled her to him.

"You were brave," he said. "Very brave. I'm proud of you."

Lou's throat tightened. She swallowed and tasted the sour, spent gunpowder.

"I think this was the Cartel. That's the only thing that makes sense."

Lou nodded. Her father rubbed his hand on her back. "You're shivering." He set down his rifle and draped his coat over her shoulders. "Are you okay?"

Lou feigned a smile and nodded. She pulled her arms into the coat. It swallowed her, but eased the chill that coursed through her body.

Her dad picked up the rifle. "Come with me."

Lou slid one of the long sleeves up to her elbow, her hand emerged beneath the cuff, and she picked up her pack. She slung it over one shoulder and then the other. It didn't sit right with the extra-large coat on her back, but there was extra padding that made up for the awkward fit.

Her father picked up his pack, draped it over one shoulder, and marched out into the street. He led Lou past the trail of bodies toward the area where he'd first opened fire.

He counted the bodies as he went. "Seven. Eight. Nine," he said. "There were more than I thought."

Lou kept her gaze straight ahead. She couldn't look at the ground despite its magnetic pull. The dead men were staring back at her, judging her, questioning her morality, as she shuffled past them. The last thing she wanted to risk was making eye contact. She quickened her pace and slid next to her father. She reached for his free hand and let him lead her through the grid of streets until they found a man in the near distance who was still alive.

It was the bearded man with the white hat. Strong and confident minutes ago, he now appeared small. He was dragging himself along the road, his clothes and boots scraping against the asphalt.

Her father stopped. They were twenty yards from the man. He motioned toward the inchworm of a man. "Is that him?"

Lou nodded.

He let go of her hand and marched ahead, his steps deliberate. He made a straight line for the dying figure and raised his rifle. He aimed for the man's head, the white hat itself, lowering the barrel as he approached.

Lou checked over one shoulder and then the other. Confident they were alone, that her father had killed the entirety of the horde save one, she followed her father. She stayed far enough away to be safe but was close enough to hear. She considered digging underneath the big coat for a knife, but didn't. Dad had this under control.

The man looked up, lifting his chin from the ground. He squinted at the rifle pointed at his face. He lowered his head again, resting the side of his face on the asphalt.

Even in the darkness Lou could make out a long, dark, irregular smudge that marked the path the man had taken to his current place. He was bleeding out.

David poked the man with the barrel of the rifle. He jerked the barrel upward and tipped the man's hat from his head. Then he jabbed it into his temple and demanded, "Who are you?"

The man exhaled; his lungs rattled. He told Lou's father what he could do to himself.

David flipped the rifle around his hand and swept the butt across the side of the man's head as if he were striking a hockey puck. Lou winced at the cracking sound of the Mossberg's black synthetic stock hitting the man's skull. She opened her mouth to say something but thought better of it.

"Who are you?" repeated her father. "Are you Cartel?"

The man grunted in short, uneven breaths. He rolled onto his back. His breath puffed in small clouds above him before quickly evaporating. David put a boot squarely on the man's chest and pushed slightly.

The man groaned, and a plume of his moist breath sprayed into the air. He coughed up something wet. When he finally spoke, his voice didn't remotely resemble the butter-smooth, resonant one Lou had heard minutes earlier. Now he sounded a hundred years old with smoker's lungs and a damaged voice box.

"Of course I'm Cartel," he rasped. "Who are you?"

Lou's father looked back at her. She took a reluctant step forward and adjusted her ball cap. She spun it so the bill was at an angle on the front of her head. She held onto it while she awaited her father's response.

"I'm about to be the man who kills you," he said. "But I could be your salvation."

"There's no saving me," he rasped. "I'm a goner. Do what you gotta do."

The man lay flat on the road and looked straight up at the sky. There was a small bald spot at the top of his head, the rest of his receding hair was matted with sweat.

David crouched next to the man and said something Lou couldn't hear. He motioned toward her with his head, but didn't look at her. His attention was on the dying man on the road.

The man's chest heaved up and down. He rolled his head back and forth on the asphalt.

David leaned in and whispered to the man.

Lou walked forward, straining to hear whatever it was he was saying to try to convince the man to offer them some sort of helpful information. She loved her father for it. He'd proven again and again that he would do anything for her, even if it first appeared to be futile.

Lou doubted the bearded man would help. He'd get the final word by not offering any.

But then he did.

He rolled his face toward David, his trembling hands motioning as he conveyed his response. The conversation lasted for several minutes. Then the man blindly reached for something Lou couldn't see. Her father obscured the view. She craned her neck and inched forward to see the man hand something to her father, placing it in his palm. The man hesitated, dragging his fingers across the object before letting go. He said something brief and rolled back to face the black, cloudless sky. A puff of breath drifted upward.

David pressed himself to his feet and stiffly walked back toward Lou. He cleared his throat and spoke as if he didn't want the man to hear him.

"He told me how to avoid the Cartel between here and the crossing into Oklahoma closest to Lawton. He told me where they've got men positioned."

Lou looked doubtful. "How would he know that?"

Her father held a finger to his lips. "He's a captain. He's in charge of this area. He said it stretches a good ways toward the Red River."

"A captain?"

"Yes. He said there are bosses too, and that we can tell them by the hats. Then there are the grunts. They don't wear hats."

"Why did he tell you that?" asked Lou. "What if he's a liar?"

Her father wrinkled his chin and considered her question. "He might be lying. But I think he's telling me the truth."

"Why?"

"He gave me something valuable," he said, "something to give to someone he loves."

Lou glanced at her father's fist. He turned it over and opened his fingers. In his palm was a simple gold band. "Is that a ring?" she asked.

"Yes."

"Whose is it?"

"It belonged to his wife. She died in the Scourge."

He held out his hand, offering it to Lou. She pinched it between her fingers and held it up. There was an inscription inside the band. It was too hard to read in the dark, but Lou could feel it with her finger.

"He asked me to give it to their daughter," said David.

Lou handed back the ring. David slid it into his hand and then stuffed it into his pocket.

"How old is she?"

"The daughter?"

"Yes."

"Nine," said her father.

Lou glanced over at the man. The puffs of air were thinner, less frequent. "He wants you to find his daughter and give her the ring?"

David nodded.

"He's telling the truth about the Cartel, isn't he?"

David looked at the man over his shoulder. Without acknowledging Lou, he walked back to the bearded man, picked the white hat up off the ground, and placed it on the man's chest, pulling his limp hands onto its wide brim to keep it there. He stood there for a couple of minutes, dropped to one knee, and brushed his fingers across the man's eyes. He picked up the white hat from the man's chest and stuffed it into the top of his pack.

Lou noticed the puffs of vapor were gone. The man's chest was still.

Her father walked back to her. He sighed. "He was telling the truth."

The knot in Lou's throat, the tightness that had lessened, expanded again. She'd killed the man. The man whose eyes had stared into hers was a father. He had a daughter just like her.

She didn't think about the fact that he'd tried to kidnap her, or worse, and that he was a leader in a gang of bad people intent on doing bad things. She focused on the paralyzing guilt swirling around in her young mind.

Lou felt the sting in her eyes as tears spilled onto her face. Despite the oversized coat covering much of her, she trembled.

Her father approached her and pulled her into his body. He absorbed her sobs and let her mourn. Lou looked up at him, and he wiped the sheen from under her eyes and nose.

"He was a dad," she said. "I killed him. I didn't have to kill him. I could have gotten away. I could have hurt him without killing him."

David listened, his eyes staying locked onto hers as she explained why the guilt was swallowing her whole. She rambled and repeated the same thoughts over and again. He waited until she stopped talking.

"Lou," he said, "sometimes I forget how young you are. You talk like a teenager; you hunt like an adult. I forget how young you are."

She sniffed and wiped her face with the arm of the coat. She stepped back, releasing her embrace.

"You're a child," David said, "and children shouldn't see such things. I've told you before I wish we could spend our time practicing penalty kicks at the Y or back handsprings at the gym."

"I know——" she started.

He raised his finger, cutting her off before she explained she'd already heard this line of thought. "But we can't. We live in an unforgiving world now. Believe me, Lou, when I tell you that it's always hard to know if you've gone overboard, if you've acted with too much force. It's easy to know when you didn't do enough."

Lou pressed her hand to her chest. Her fingers gripped the coat fabric. "He had a girl like me. I killed somebody's dad."

David sucked in a deep breath, his chest expanding with what appeared to be frustration. He exhaled through pursed lips, the vapor streaming like smoke into the air between them.

"I can't take away what you feel," he said. "I can tell you this, though. If you hadn't taken that girl's father from her, he would have taken you from me."

Lou loosened her grip on the wad of coat in her hand. She rubbed her hand across the front to smooth the fabric.

Her dad put his finger under her chin and lifted her head. He stared into her eyes and spoke with firm clarity. "You are going to kill people up until the day someone kills you. You need to think that way. You need to understand that this is survival of the fittest. Period. You cannot trust anyone. You cannot be weak. You cannot let guilt or remorse consume you."

Lou swallowed hard. The knot was shrinking, but it was still there.

"I don't expect you to grasp all of this right now. You're too young, despite how old you seem to be. If I repeat it enough, though, it'll sink in eventually."

"Where is she?" Lou asked.

David's brow furrowed with confusion. "Who?"

"The girl."

"Oh, she's in San Angelo."

"Then that's where we need to go," said Lou. "We need to give her the ring."

"What about Oklahoma? Our plan was to cross the wall before it's finished and get out of here."

"You say all the time that plans change."

"True."

"Then we should go to San Angelo. *Then* we can go to Oklahoma."

David sighed. "It's not exactly on the way."

"Nothing is on the way," she said. "Everything is a mess. You said it."

"You're good at using my own words against me. I'll have to be more careful about what I say."

"I'm incorrigible."

David laughed and drew his daughter to him. He put his hand on the back of her head and kissed the top of her cap. "I love you, Lou."

"I love you too, Dad."

David started walking. "San Angelo, it is."

CHAPTER 12

It was more than two hundred miles on foot to San Angelo. It was southwest of Archer City, essentially in the opposite direction of Lawton, Oklahoma. They'd traveled primarily on US Highway 277, taking occasional detours for water and for safety. As they entered San Angelo, they'd cut east and then entered town walking south along Texas 208. David had a specific destination in mind.

Arriving in San Angelo marked the end of a taxing journey that David tweaked and changed as they moved. He was always consulting his ragged map, guessing at the safest path to their destination. After the deadly confrontation in Archer City, he was more determined than ever to avoid accidental contact with anyone, let alone the Cartel. The trip was anything but a straight line. They never camped less than a mile from the main route. It turned a six-day trip, walking twelve hours a day, into nearly nine.

Lou and David had managed to settle into a routine. They were up before dawn with enough time to eat and break camp before hitting the road. They'd walk for six hours and take a break to go to the bathroom and rest. Then they'd walk another six hours, hunting for food during the last four to five miles, and set up camp.

Lou had become proficient at kindling a fire with dead leaves, dry sticks, and a flint starter. She could skin any game blindfolded and could pitch a tent as fast as her dad.

Along the way they talked about the way the world had been and how it had become the dystopia it was now. Her dad would summarize the plots of his favorite movies and books, careful not to spoil the endings of the novels he wanted her to read someday.

He'd quiz her on anatomy, the periodic table, and the state capitals. Lou questioned the necessity of any of it. David had explained that knowledge was never unnecessary, and it was one of the few things one could never have too much of. Lou guessed that the other things were love, money, and .556-caliber bullets. He'd added health and food to her list but told her she was otherwise absolutely right.

After a week, their nightly routine included blister checks and bandage repairs. It didn't matter how many pairs of socks Lou wore or how she adjusted her boots, the amount of walking they did each day was bound to wear against her insoles and heels.

Lou could swear she was growing too. Even without extra socks, her boots were snugger than she remembered. Her pant legs were shorter, and her shirt was bunching at her armpits. She dreaded the idea of having to find new clothing, so she didn't say anything to her dad. If he didn't notice it, she wouldn't bring it up. Life was tough enough without having to shop for clothing.

She'd never been to San Angelo. It wasn't the kind of place someone puts on their bucket list, even when the end of the world is visible on the horizon. Her dad had been there before for business. The Texas Department of Transportation, where he'd worked, had a construction and maintenance office there. It was a nondescript, white and cream-colored collection of one-story buildings with green metal roofs. It was on the northern edge of the city, and taking

Highway 208 meant they had very little contact with any of the remaining population.

Aside from an abandoned tire service business and a handful of houses set back off the road's west side, they didn't even approach any buildings. It was the perfect way to get into town unnoticed.

As they approached the compound, David joked with her about the town, suggesting it was the opposite of New York City, another place Lou had never been.

"It's a great place to live," he said of San Angelo, "but I wouldn't want to visit."

They walked to the side of the complex and a series of connecting parking lots adjacent to the green-roofed buildings. He pointed ahead and led her with the confidence of someone who knew exactly where he was going.

"I do remember a great Tex-Mex place," he said. "It wasn't too far from here. Franco's Cafe. They had good lunch specials. Another place, Heff's Burgers, was the best. I loved eating there. They used to have a deal where if you bought fries and a drink, you'd get the burger for free."

"You're making me hungry," Lou griped, stepping over a cracked concrete parking bumper. "I don't even remember what a hamburger tastes like."

"Sorry. I won't talk about food. But I do remember staying at a cool hotel called Pearl on the Concho. It had an indoor courtyard with an indoor pool. The rooms surrounded it. Smelled like chlorine when you left your room, but it was a nice atmosphere, and on a government travel budget, it wasn't too bad."

"Con-cho," said Lou. "Weird name."

"It's the name of a river that runs through town. The Concho River meanders through the city and into a lake to the southwest."

"Where are we meandering?" she asked with a grin.

"You'll see. Almost there."

He led her across the third connected parking lot until they reached a door on the back side of the main building. David stepped up to the door and handed Lou his rifle. "Hold this. I think I remember the code."

Lou's eyes widened. "They have power?"

He shook his head. "No. The coded lock isn't electronic, it's mechanical. It's old and it should work if the code hasn't changed."

Lou stepped to one side so she could get a better look at the lock. It was a rectangular stainless-steel box that had a stainless round knob protruding from it at its base. Above the knob, inset in a single column, were five stainless buttons.

Her father bent down to look at the buttons and closed his eyes. He punched a combination of the buttons. Six punches. Then he turned the knob. It didn't open. He cursed under his breath.

"Can't remember it?" asked Lou.

David clenched his jaw and shook his head. He held up a finger, suggesting now was not a good time for a conversation. He tried another combination and turned the handle. It didn't work.

Lou resisted the urge to ask if she could try it. Of course, she didn't know the combination, but she was ten years old. She wanted to play with it.

Her father tried again with a combination slightly different than the previous two. He paused and exhaled. He looked back at Lou and tried the knob. It spun. He drove his shoulder into the heavy door and pushed.

"Yes!" he said triumphantly and motioned Lou into the hallway beyond the door. The door shut and left them in the dark. "Give it a second," he said. "Once our eyes adjust a bit, I can guide us to a good room where we can catch some sleep."

Lou handed back the Mossberg. "Why did they use that kind of lock?"

"Two reasons. You don't need a key and you don't need power. Some of the important work TxDOT did was in bad weather, when there wasn't any power. They had to have access to the buildings, but

TOM ABRAHAMS

they didn't want keys floating around out there. They get lost, get copied."

Lou blinked a couple of times and was better able to see her surroundings. They were in a long corridor. There was a solid floor and a low ceiling made of light-colored tile squares. The hallway was narrow, and it appeared there were a couple of doors on either side.

"I'm ready," she said.

David took her hand and led her along the corridor. Their boots squeaked on the floor as they moved. The place had a distinct odor that was familiar, but Lou couldn't quite place it. It reminded her of old people. Her father tugged her along to the last door on the left, where he stopped and opened the door. It creaked open and they stepped into a room noticeably cooler than the hallway. It was actually cold.

David reached into his jacket. It was the one Lou had worn for a couple of days before giving it back, finding it too uncomfortable hiking in an oversized coat. He pulled a palm-sized LED flashlight from the pocket and pushed the power button. It didn't work. He shook the flashlight in his hand and then thumped it with his palm a couple of times. When he pushed the button again, it flickered on and cast a bright white cone of light across the room.

As he swept the beam across the room, dust dancing and swirling in the light, Lou knew why her father had picked this spot. It was perfect.

Along the far wall was a large overstuffed and plush fabric sofa. To its left, in the corner, there was an end table with a useless lamp atop it. The table separated a second identical sofa. It reminded her of the river home in Marble Falls they'd reluctantly left weeks earlier.

Her father scanned the room with the light, revealing the industrial Berber carpet on the floor and the wet bar to the far right. The bar was adorned with a coffee maker and a microwave. There was even a small refrigerator, its doors hanging open. Thankfully it

100

was empty. If not, the rot and the stench would have made the place untenable.

David gave the room one more pass and then aimed the light at the first sofa. "We should be safe here. We're locked inside. We have a comfortable place to rest up. Only downfall is the darkness. There aren't any windows in the break room."

Lou followed the light to the sofa and jumped onto it. She bounced on its worn spring cushions and shrugged off her pack. She untucked the knives from her waist and set them on the table in the corner.

"That didn't take any convincing." David chuckled. "I guess someone is ready for bed, even though it's late afternoon and we haven't eaten dinner yet."

"We can eat tomorrow," said Lou. "My feet hurt, my neck hurts, I'm cold, and I'm sleepy."

"Okay. We'll eat tomorrow."

He pivoted and aimed the beam at the other sofa. He crossed the room and sat down with a heavy sigh, grunted off his own pack, and laid the rifle on the floor in front of the sofa, tucking the business end under the furniture and toward the wall.

He pulled off his boots and set them next to Lou's. Then he flicked off the flashlight and the room was again bathed in darkness. David started talking to Lou about what the day ahead might hold, but she was already drifting off to sleep. All she heard was "hornet's nest" before she was out.

***

Lou opened her eyes in a panic and sat up straight, bracing herself with locked elbows. Her hands sank into the worn sofa cushions, and she searched the darkness for some clue as to where she was. Rivulets of cold sweat dripped from her forehead. The dampness coated the back of her neck, under her hair, and the small of her back. She licked her lips and tasted the briny beads of perspiration.

Her pulse was thumping against her chest, neck, and temples. She reached for her hip with one hand. Her knife wasn't there. She groped around in the dark, unable to see beyond the end of her nose or gather any intelligence as to where she was or why.

Her fingers dragged along the smooth synthetic fabric of the sofa, and she spun to plant her feet on the floor. The Berber was rough on her heels and toes.

She started to push herself from the sofa when she heard a familiar sound, the rumbling motor of a snore.

Dad.

He was to her right and still asleep.

Then she remembered. She was in the break room of the regional TxDOT office in San Angelo—a place great to call home, not so great to visit.

Truth was, she thought as she regained control of her breathing and wiped the sheen of sweat from her face, no place was any good to visit anymore. No place was good enough to call home.

The post-Scourge world was essentially a no-man's-land. Lou sank back into the sofa and pulled her legs to her chest. She hugged her knees and curled her toes under her feet.

She wanted to wake her father up and ask him if they would ever be able to stop running. Even if they went north of the wall to Oklahoma, would they settle down? Would they be able to have a place to call home?

She didn't understand that the lack of someplace to ground her life was the reason she woke up in a panic. At her age she couldn't comprehend that uncertainty was the reason she lived with the nagging sense of dread in the back of her mind.

She did know she was tired, already, of the nightmares. She was weary of the long walks to somewhere no better than the place they'd left. She tightened her hold on her legs and grumbled to herself about Earlene and Teddy. She wished they'd never come home. She wished they'd stayed at their ranch in Hallettsville. She wished, before taking it back and asking God to forgive her, that the Cartel had killed them. If they'd died, they'd never have arrived at the river house, and she and her father would still be living peacefully in Marble Falls.

She tried to erase the thought from her mind, tried to push it into the corner with the rest of the guilt that threatened to consume her young mind. She distracted herself by calling out to her father.

"Dad?"

He snorted but didn't answer her. The springs creaked under his body. He must have shifted his weight to get more comfortable. She called him again, more loudly.

"Dad?"

He muttered something unintelligible. Then he cleared his throat and snorted again. "Yeah?"

Lou sighed. "I was just making sure you were there, that's all. I didn't know where we are."

The springs creaked under his weight. Lou could hear him moving on the sofa, followed by a click and the sound of her father shaking something. Then the bright cone of LED light beamed from the flashlight. He swept it across the room until he found Lou.

She shielded her eyes from the light, squinting against it. "Dad," she protested.

He moved the beam. "Sorry. I'm still out of it. You okay?"

"Fine." Lou held out her flattened hand and tilted it back and forth. "Do you know what time it is? How long have we been asleep?"

"I don't know. My guess is it's probably late morning. We easily slept more than twelve hours. My stomach is growling."

Lou touched her stomach. There were familiar hunger pangs, but nothing she hadn't had before. Even a skewered squirrel or rabbit every night wasn't enough to satiate her hunger. She could eat. But more importantly, she wanted to get the ring back to the dead Cartel captain's daughter. She alternately curled and extended her toes. The rough Berber felt good.

"Can we eat after we return the ring?" she asked. "I'd like to give her the ring before we do anything else. We should get the ring to her."

Her dad flicked off the light. "About that," he said. "It's not going to be as easy as walking up and handing it to her."

Lou pulled her feet back up onto the sofa, her heels pressing on the front edge of the cushion. She took off her cap, ran her fingers through her greasy hair, and then put the cap back on her head. She thought about asking her father why, but knew if she was quiet, he'd tell her anyway.

"I know her name," he said. "I know she's here in San Angelo. She's supposed to be in one of the Cartel hangouts near the river."

"Then let's go to the hangout and ask for her. They'll let us give her the ring."

Lou didn't realize how naïve she remained. Despite everything she'd seen and done, there was something in her that wanted to believe the best in people, even the Cartel.

"It doesn't work that way, Lou. It could be dangerous."

Lou bristled. "Then why did we come here if we can't give her the ring?"

The sofa creaked and David stood up. Lou could hear the semi-arthritic joints in his knees crack before he plopped onto the sofa next to her. She bounced a bit against the springs.

"I didn't say we couldn't do it," he said, his body leaning against hers. "I said it wasn't easy and it could be dangerous."

"How dangerous?"

David flicked on the light, shining it on his own face. It gave him a ghastly appearance, which Lou thought might be his reasoning for doing it, and highlighted the look of concern on his face. It answered her question, but it didn't frighten her.

"What's her name?" she asked.

"Sarah Jane Newman."

"Sarah Jane," repeated Lou. "Sarah. Jane."

"Her mother was Rachel. Her father was Scull Newman."

Lou let that last name roll around in her head. The man she'd killed, the father of a girl her age, was named Scull. Scull Newman. Now she had a name to go with the bearded man's pain-etched face.

"I'll do it," she said.

Her dad shifted away from her and shone the light on her face. "Do what, Louise?"

"Dad, please don't call me Louise," she said, shielding her eyes from the direct beam.

He moved the light. "Do what?" he repeated.

"I'll take her the ring."

David chuckled condescendingly. "How do you figure? It would be a cold day in Hell before I let you deliver the ring."

"Dad, do I have permission to cuss?"

"Okay," he said tentatively.

"It is cold," she said. "And we're in Hell."

He chuckled again, but Lou recognized it as a different laugh. The condescension was gone, replaced by nervousness.

He steeled his voice. "I won't allow it."

Lou bit the inside of her cheek, resisting the urge to plead her case. She knew it wouldn't do her any good. The art of subtlety was beyond her but manipulation was not. The more her father talked, the more he'd make her points for her.

"I'm not letting you walk into the hornet's nest alone," he said. "Not going to happen. There are too many things that can go wrong."

Lou leaned back, sinking in the corner between the back cushion and the wide padded arm. She curled her legs underneath her, tucking her cold feet into the space between the cushions.

"You're ten years old," he said. "I know Sarah Jane is nine years old, but it's not like you can walk in there pretending to be friends with her."

Lou cleared her throat. Twice.

"Even if you could get to her," he said, "even if she didn't care that you lied to get to her, you then have to explain how you got the ring, how you know who she is and how you found her."

"I could lie again," Lou said. "I want to give her the ring. If I have to lie two times to do it, it's okay."

"Then you have to get out of there without the Cartel snatching you up. I don't see it."

"What's your plan?" she asked. "What do you want to do?"

"I don't know," David admitted. "It's not like I'll be able to waltz on in there either. They're not going to let a grown man mosey up to a little girl inside a Cartel stronghold."

Lou giggled.

"What's funny?"

"You said mosey."

"I did, didn't I?" David chuckled. "I guess I'm unwittingly adapting to our environment. I'll have to watch that."

Lou tucked her hands under her armpits. Her fingers were cold and getting stiff. She mouthed the word *mosey* again and smiled to herself. It wasn't the time for joking around, but she couldn't help herself with such a silly word.

Mosey.

"That leaves us with one option," David said, "unless you've changed your mind about delivering the ring. We could leave it somewhere and hope she gets it. Then we could head out."

Lou scowled at him. She knew he couldn't see the expression on her face, but she figured her silence did the trick.

"Then we have to do it together," he reasoned. "It's not the best option. That would be forgoing this mission altogether. But I've got an idea about how we can do this together."

"Then let's do it," she said.

***

The sun hit Lou like a thousand LED flashlights when she emerged from the TxDot building. The sun was lower in the sky than she'd imagined it would be, but it hit her square in the eyes as she walked out. Her dad stepped outside and pulled the white hat from his pack. He gently put his fist inside of it, punched it to re-shape it, and set it atop his head. He smiled at Lou and tipped the hat as if he were greeting her in passing. She raised an eyebrow but didn't say anything. He motioned toward the sun.

"It must be three o'clock," he said. "That only gives us a few hours before it starts to get dark. We're not doing this in the dark."

Lou snapped the chest strap together at her belly, and it tightened her pack against her back. She'd wanted to leave it inside the break room, figuring they'd come back and sleep again before heading out the next day. Her dad, however, had told her there was a distinct possibility they'd be running from town after delivering the ring. They couldn't afford to leave anything behind.

She adjusted the straps on her sore shoulders and made sure her knives were easily accessible under her shirt. They were tucked at her hips inside thin leather sheaths that hung from a thin, knotted belt she wore low on her narrow hips.

She slid the blades up and down a couple of times to make sure they were easily drawable if the situation called for a fast, violent response. She prayed that wouldn't be needed. With the bloody image of the bearded Scull Newman plastered in her mind's eye, the last thing she wanted was more death.

She followed her father along the empty streets. They clung to the sidewalks, keeping close to the low-slung buildings dotting the streets. As they moved closer to the river, the density increased. So did the population. Lou felt the eyes of women and children following them as they passed open windows or stepped by covered porches.

The wary eyes glared suspiciously at them from under the shade of the metal awnings that protruded from the fronts of old shops and restaurants. None of them said anything, though, and Lou knew well enough to avoid eye contact.

They were a couple of blocks from the river when her dad stopped. He eyed a sheepish-looking man sweeping clean the stained pine planks that led into his building. It was a deck that stretched ten feet square. The boards were warped, the stain was faded, and there were nail pops that made stepping onto the deck an awkward task.

Still, Lou followed her dad onto the edge of the deck. The man stopped sweeping. He white-knuckled the broom handle and averted his eyes as Lou's father ran his finger along the brim of the white hat with one hand and balanced the Mossberg in the other.

"I'm looking for Sarah Jane Newman," he said.

The man wrung his hands on the broom handle and shot a look at Lou before he spoke. His long face was accentuated by sad, drooping eyes, which hid behind heavy lids. His receding hairline drew back as he appeared to consider whether or not he should answer the question truthfully.

"You know her?" Her father took another step closer to the man, invading his space. The man shuffled back a step.

"Sarah. Jane. Newman," her father repeated in a tone that she rarely heard him employ. It was forceful but restrained, as if he were asking her to do her chores for the third time. He was frustrated, but hadn't yet lost his cool.

The man lowered his head as he spoke. His voice was above a whisper and he mumbled. Lou couldn't hear what he said.

"Speak up," ordered her father.

The man raised his voice and spoke quickly. "Miss Hattie's Museum," he said. "On Concho."

"Miss Hattie's," her father repeated. It wasn't a question. It was more of a response barbed with disbelief.

"On Concho," said the man. His hands were trembling now. It

was evident in the broom bristles vibrating against the warped pine. "The museum. The building just east of the old bookshop."

"You know her?"

The man's face twitched. "Yes. Everybody knows her. She's Scull Newman's daughter. Everybody knows Scull Newman."

The man glanced at the hat atop Lou's father's head. His eyes blinked and his mouth curled downward.

David nodded. "Who else is there?"

The man tilted his head to one side as if he didn't understand the question. His wiry, unkempt eyebrows squeezed together. His heavy lids made his eyes almost disappear.

"You're a captain," he said with a hint of doubt. "I figured you would—"

David put both hands on his rifle, but he kept it aimed at the deck. "This isn't my area," he snapped. "I don't know the inhabitants of every building between here and Harris County."

The man shook his head in apology and backed up. "I didn't know. I—"

"Answer the question," David ordered, raising his voice.

Lou checked over her shoulder. Others had stopped whatever they were doing to watch the show. Clearly, they'd seen scenes like this before. When she caught their eyes, they averted them, acting as though they were otherwise occupied.

"It's for orphans," he explained. "Well, I mean, not orphans. Kids whose moms are dead and whose dads are away in the Cartel. That's where they stay."

"They have adults watching them?"

The man nodded. His shoulder curled inward and he hunched over. "They have some grunts watching over them. All the time."

"Good," said David. "Now get back to work. Keep this place spotless, hear?"

The man bowed and returned to sweeping. David turned and stepped purposefully from the deck with his shoulders back. He hopped to the street and pointed south with his rifle.

"Let's go," he said.

"He thought you were a captain?" Lou asked, hurrying to keep pace.

Her dad shrugged. "Seems so. The hat did the trick."

"What's Miss Hattie's Museum?"

"I don't know. I never did much sightseeing here. Work, dinner, and sleep. That was about it."

As they neared a tall building on their left, Lou's dad gripped her by the arm. Startled, she gasped and looked up at him. He winked at her and told her, loudly, to keep up. It was then Lou noticed the collection of men gathered in front of the building underneath its rusting awning. All of them eyed Lou and her dad as they hurried past.

The building was marked with the faded outline of large lettering that once spelled out THE CACTUS HOTEL. Its front door was held open with a brick. The men leaned against the wall and sat in tattered recliners. One of the men jumped up and moved quickly toward the street.

"Who you got there?" he called as he approached. He wore the brown hat of a posse boss and was missing the lower part of one ear. Two other men left the front of the hotel and joined the man in his pursuit.

"She won't tell me who she is," David snarled. He tugged on her arm. Lou winced at his bruising grip. "I'm taking her to Miss Hattie's."

"She's a young one," said the man with the hat. "Where'd you find her?"

Lou's father slowed to a stop but kept his arm around Lou's bicep. He snorted and then spat onto the street. "North of town. A couple of miles from here."

The man adjusted his brown hat on his head and then tucked his thumbs into his jeans pockets. He looked Lou's father up and down.

"I don't know you," he said. "I mean, you got a white hat and all. I guess you're important, but I don't know you."

David chuckled. "I don't know you either. But I do know you and your grunts here best not keep talking to me like I ain't your superior."

"If this ain't your area, then you ain't my superior," the boss said.

Lou's father let go of her arm and jabbed a finger at her chest. "You stay while I deal with this. You run, I shoot."

Lou played along. She lowered her head and stood in place.

David took two defiant steps toward the boss and stared at him. "You were saying something about my authority?"

The man shrugged. "I just find it interesting that you and your little girl there have matching packs, but you say you just found her. Plus, you look alike. Brown skin, same eyes."

"What's your name?" asked David, ignoring the boss's observations. "I need to have a talk with Scull about you."

The man's cracked lips spread into a smile the way an inchworm stretches its body when moving. He scratched the thick patch of black stubble on his chin. Then he stepped closer to David. The two men were inches apart now. Lou felt the tension roil in her gut. She counted the number of men in the street. There were four plus the boss.

Even if she quickly unloaded a pair of accurate strikes, hitting two men almost simultaneously, and her father took out the boss, that left two more grunts. All of the men were armed. Three had shotguns, and two had sidearms. It was not a favorable situation. Even a ten-year-old could see that.

Still, she slid her hands from underneath her pack's shoulder straps and lowered them to her sides. Unconsciously she fluttered her fingers as would a piano player tapping notes in the air.

The posse boss, the wormy smile still bridging his cheeks, rested his hand on the top of his holstered handgun. He stepped back from David without losing eye contact.

"Bogan," he said. "Tell Scull you talked to Bogan."

"That your first name or last name?" asked David, undeterred by the thickening tension or the quintet of armed men in front of them.

"Don't matter," said Bogan. "Scully'll know who I am. I work for him, not you, remember?"

David narrowed his eyes. "We all work for Roof, don't we?"

Bogan's smile disappeared. David took another step back and spun toward Lou. He took her arm, more gently than before.

"Let's go," he said and tugged her past the crowd. They'd taken a couple of steps when Bogan called after them.

"Hey, Captain," he said. "How many generals we got, not counting Roof on account of you already mentioned him?"

David stopped. His fingers squeezed her bicep. Lou looked up at him. His eyes were closed. He was exhaling slowly, the vapor of his breath a steady stream into the cold late afternoon air. Despite their having traveled south, the weather hadn't warmed.

That would mean her father's joints were stiffer than they would be otherwise. His draw wouldn't have the same snap. He'd be a beat slower than he'd have been in the sweaty, humid summer months, and it would take him time to pull the rifle into both of his hands. By then, he'd be shot at least once if not dead.

"I asked you a question," said Bogan.

Lou's pulse quickened. Her face felt flush and she was short of breath. She closed her eyes and tried to calm herself.

David exhaled.

The sound of Velcro scratching and the slide being pulled back to chamber a round preceded what Lou imagined would be his final warning. She didn't have to see him to know his handgun was a nine-millimeter. She wondered why he didn't already have it ready. Perhaps it was for effect.

"Hey," said Bogan. "You suddenly go deaf? I want to—"

Lou's father let go of her arm and at the same time spun her around behind him and whipped the Mossberg above her head. As she disappeared behind him, he flung the rifle at Bogan. It helicoptered the short distance, hitting the boss squarely in the chest. It knocked him off balance, giving David enough time to draw his .38. He quickly unloaded a pair of shots into Bogan and then a single shot at the shotgun-wielding grunt next to him.

Despite her aversion to more violence, Lou slipped into a subconscious self-preservation. The world slowed around her as she unsheathed both blades. She moved to her father's left, the side opposite his shooting hand, and ran forward two steps before planting a boot on the cracked asphalt and jumping skyward. She spotted two men behind Bogan, who was now on his knees and gripping his bleeding neck.

She whipped the first blade from her right hand, hitting the man as he unleashed a shotgun blast that was too far away from her or her father to do any damage. The blade sliced into his thigh, sticking there above the knee. It dropped the man to the ground, and he lost the shotgun as he grappled with the instant burst of pain Lou knew she'd inflicted.

The second the first blade was in the air, she switched the second knife from her left hand to her right. She landed on the ground, rolled forward, her pack making the somersault awkward, and backhanded the blade at her second target as she rose onto one knee.

It stuck into the man's side. He'd still failed to fire a shot when she hit him, but the shock of the strike forced his finger to squeeze the trigger. The stray shot flew harmlessly into the air.

While she'd taken care of two men, her father had hit the final grunt with a single shot to the head. The man dropped where he stood, his pistol skittering across the road toward Lou. She picked it up and aimed it the man with the blade in his knee. She shot his other leg and then his shoulder.

She pivoted and put a single bullet in the right arm of the grunt with the knife in his side. He cried out in pain and passed out, his head cracking against the asphalt.

David descended on the carnage and removed the weapons one at a time, picking them up and cradling them in his arms. "Lou, get the Mossberg."

She handed her father the semi-automatic and rose to her feet, stepped over a body, and withdrew the knife from the first target's knee. It didn't loosen easily. She had to use her boot heel to help pry it free. The grunt's body responded limply.

She moved past him to retrieve the second knife. She grasped the handle and slid it from the man's side, wiped both blades on the man's pants, and replaced them into the leather pouches on her hips. She maneuvered through the arms, legs, and torsos and picked up the Mossberg.

David had emptied the remaining ammo from all of the Cartel's weapons and scattered it in an alley across the street from the hotel. He waved Lou toward him and began walking farther south.

Lou held the rifle with both hands and jogged to catch up with her father. She noticed he was tossing one weapon after the other down side streets, flinging them as far as he could.

The pack swung on her back as she hustled, the chest strap tugging against her ribs. "Dad," she huffed when she caught up to him, "what do we do?"

He moved double-time, his long legs stretching as he walked quickly south. Having tossed the last of the shotguns to the side, he tucked a dull gray semi-automatic pistol into the front of his pants and took the Mossberg from Lou. "We keep moving. We're not going to have much time at the museum. Those gunshots will draw attention. People saw us. They'll point the bad guys in the right direction."

Lou tried glancing over her shoulder as she moved, but the pack prevented a good look at anything. Her lower back ached, her shoulders hurt, and the underside of her ribs was getting sore. "Maybe it wasn't a good idea to give her the ring," she said between labored breaths. "Maybe we—"

"Don't think it," her father said, leading her around a corner. "It's the right thing to do. It's worth the risk if it gives you peace of mind."

Lou wasn't so sure of that, but it was too late to do anything about it. Twice now they'd experienced the vile nature of the Cartel. Twice now they'd been fortunate to escape unscathed. Not many men, like her father, would have the skill to do what he'd done. She imagined not many, if any, girls her age would have the gymnastics background and the innate skills in the impalement arts as she. Absent that, the Cartel would have won both times.

Lou wondered if either of the men she'd attacked this time were fathers. They appeared too young. But she'd consciously worked to disable them without killing them. She had no way of knowing if the knife or bullet wounds would kill them; they could bleed out or get nasty, ultimately fatal infections. Still, at least she'd tried to leave them alive.

It wasn't something she'd planned. There was no planning for that scuffle. It was a split-second decision she'd made as she whipped the blades and pulled the trigger. It was better to wonder if they'd survived than to know they were dead.

Her dad had once told her a story about a cat in a sealed box. As long as the box was closed, it was possible the cat was alive. The minute the box opened, the cat's fate became apparent. The philosophical argument was that whoever opened the box ultimately determined whether the cat lived or died. Lou didn't understand how opening the box killed the cat or gave it life. She didn't remember the name of the philosopher either, even though her dad had repeated it throughout the story.

She did, however, think of those two men as cats in a box. It made it easier to push the violence from her mind as they reached the front of Miss Hattie's Museum. Lou read the faded signage above the front entrance, mouthing the words.

"Dad?" she asked. "What's a brothel?"

David scratched the back of his neck. "Ask me later."

Miss Hattie's Museum, now a boardinghouse for the single-parent children of Cartel grunts, bosses, and captains, was originally a house of ill repute.

For fifty years the building was one of the many bordellos on Concho Avenue. It was shut down for the final time by the Texas Rangers in 1952, some eighty years before Lou and her father stepped through its doorway. The decor hadn't changed much, as it had been preserved as a museum that drew only the occasional tourist before the Scourge.

Now, given its large number of rooms and accompanying beds, it was the perfect boardinghouse for children awaiting the return of the Cartel fathers. If the information the skinny broom sweeper had given them was correct, one of those children was Sarah Jane Newman.

The sun-wrinkled grunt at the front door didn't question Lou's father when he told him he was there to see Scull Newman's kid. The man swung the door open and motioned for Lou and David to step inside; then he stepped into the ornately adorned blood-red and gold room. Sitting to one side on a chenille love seat was a dowdy woman with a nest of hair pinned into a loose bun atop her head. She was reading a book with the name Nabokov on the spine. Lou couldn't see the title. When they entered, she closed the book and looked up at her visitors, keeping her index finger between the pages to mark her spot. Her skin was pale, nearly translucent, and a permanent frown dominated her features. Her thick, slug-shaped lips curled downward. Her eyes were too small for her face and were set close together above her tiny pug nose.

Her appearance was so odd, Lou couldn't stop looking at her, transfixed by her surreal, cartoonish appearance. Her squeaky voice only added to the entertainment of it.

"Can I help you?"

"They're here to see Sarah Jane Newman," the grunt said. "They have something for her."

The woman's eyebrows stretched upward. She cracked open the book and set it on a mahogany coffee table in front of her. "Is that so?" She stood up, attempting to press the wrinkles from her dress. "What do you have?"

"It's from her dad," said Lou. "It's something that belonged to him."

The woman's brows lowered. Her frown deepened and her beady eyes narrowed. "Belonged?"

"He's dead," David said flatly. "Archer City."

The woman's face didn't react to the news. "I see. And he entrusted you with this mission? He asked you to deliver his last will and testament to his daughter?"

"Yes," Lou answered. "My dad here was with him when he died. Captain Newman asked him to find Sarah Jane."

"Did he now?"

Lou's father put down his rifle, leaning it against a chair, and reached into his pocket. He withdrew the ring and held it up between his thumb and index finger. Then he extended his hand to the woman. She didn't take it.

Keeping her eyes on Lou and her father, she called out, "Sarah Jane." Her shrill, high-pitched voice pierced the still air of the parlor. "I need you here, please."

She motioned with her head for the grunt to go find her. He hustled from the parlor to the long hallway that stretched to the back of the museum. While they waited, Lou surveyed the parlor's interior.

The red velour curtains were pulled back from the many windows with thick decorative rope that allowed in enough light to counteract the deep red hue that dominated the space. The ceiling was unstained, decorative wood. The walls were covered in large oriental rugs that hung as tapestries. Regardless of the lack of electricity, gilded lamps stood as sentinels beside each of the seating areas: the love seat from which the housemother arose, a set of Victorian chairs with backs upholstered in faded fleur-de-lis, and a longer sofa with a high, straight back that appeared as uncomfortable now as it likely had eight decades earlier.

The woman stood with her hands clasped in front of her. Lou noticed the dress wasn't only wrinkled, despite the woman's efforts to uncrease it. It was stained in various shades of food: browns, reds, greens. The woman, or someone, had obviously worked hard to clean the frock, but hand washing was difficult, and some stains wouldn't come out. Blood, Lou knew from experience, was especially tough.

Lou, David, and the woman stood in awkward silence until the man reappeared at the end of the dark hallway a few minutes later, a smaller, frailer figure walking beside him. The man hurried the other person along, gently coaxing her into the parlor.

"These are the people here to see you," said the grunt as they entered the room. He had his hands on the girl's shoulders. Lou recognized her immediately. Sarah Jane had her father's eyes.

The woman cleared her throat. "Sarah Jane," she said firmly, "come here, please."

The girl, her eyes now fixed to the floor in front of her feet, diligently crossed the wooden floor. Her bare feet stepped onto the threadbare rug that held the coffee table, and she walked to the woman's side, her hands clasped behind her back. Her toes were curled under her feet. Her long stringy blond hair was parted down the middle of her head and draped onto both sides of her large ears. She stood taller than Lou by several inches but somehow appeared smaller. She was certainly thinner than Lou, less muscular. Her cotton dress hung on her in a way that revealed her clavicles and shoulder joints.

The woman put one hand on her shoulder, and the girl flinched before steadying herself. Her toes uncurled from underneath her feet and flexed against the rug.

"This man and his…" the woman began.

"Daughter," said David.

"This man and his *daughter*," she continued, "have traveled here on behalf of your father."

The girl's eyes brightened. A thick weight settled against Lou's chest.

"They have brought you something and asked permission to give it to you."

"Shouldn't we sit down?" asked David. "It might be good if we sat."

"We're fine as we are," said the woman. "Go ahead."

The girl craned her neck, looking straight up to eye the housemother. Her windpipe stretched against her nearly translucent skin.

"Can I have it?" she asked, her voice soft and sweet. "Please?"

The woman's eyes drifted downward and she nodded. She patted Sarah Jane's shoulder, which must have been the signal for her to move, because the girl crossed the short distance to Lou and extended her hand.

"I'm Sarah Jane," she said. A shy smile followed her salutation.

Lou took the girl's bony, cold hand in hers and shook it firmly. "I'm Lou." There was no cheer in her voice.

"Nice to meet you, Lou." The girl sidestepped to Lou's dad and again held out her hand. "I'm Sarah Jane," she repeated.

"I'm Dave." Her hand disappeared inside his as he gently shook it.

"Nice to meet you, Captain Dave," she said. She clasped her hands behind her back. She blinked at them expectantly. "My father sent me a gift?"

David opened his left hand, revealing the ring. He extended it toward the girl. Her smile evaporated when she saw it. Her eyes narrowed, as if her mind couldn't process what it was. Then they widened with recognition and darted between Lou's father, Lou, the housemother, and the ring. She took a step back. Her eyes welled. Her chin quivered.

"He wanted you to have it," said Lou. "He said it belonged to your mom."

The girl's body trembled as if a shock wave had started at her narrow shoulders and traveled down her body. She took another wobbly step back and leaned against the housemother for balance. The woman stood rigid, providing no comfort at all.

Sarah Jane blinked away the tears that began streaming silently down her cheeks and inhaled a ragged breath. A bubble of spit popped in her mouth as she spoke. "He's dead."

"He was brave," said Lou. "He—"

"Let your father speak," interrupted the housemother. "He's the one in command."

David took off his hat and held it at his chest. He smiled empathetically at Sarah Jane and then glared at the housemother. "Don't speak to my daughter like that," he said flatly. "Go ahead, Lou. You're doing just fine."

The woman scowled. Lou didn't think it possible for her frown to become any more pronounced than it was, but it did. She swallowed hard and sucked in a deep breath through her nose. Lou thought steam might blast from her ears as she began again.

"He told us about your mother," Lou explained. "He also said how much he loved you. He wanted to make sure you got the ring. I—we—wanted to get it to you."

Lou plucked the ring from her father's hand and stepped to the girl. It wasn't something she'd planned on doing, but it felt right. When she reached Sarah Jane, she wrapped her arms around her and squeezed. The girl's arms dangled at her sides for a moment before she raised them and held the sides of Lou's pack.

The girl sobbed and Lou's stomach lurched. Her vision blurred and she too started crying. She sniffed back the tears and pulled away from Sarah Jane. She took one of her hands and handed her the ring, folding the girl's fingers around the gold band.

Sarah Jane took the ring and held it tight in her hand. She opened her mouth to say something when the door to the museum burst open. A burly man with a sweat-stained white long-sleeved T-shirt was breathless. He held a shotgun at his side. A belt loaded with shells hung loosely at his waist. He yelled to the grunt in the parlor.

"We gotta go," he said as he stepped inside. "Somebody killed Bogan and a bunch of his men over at the old Cactus. He was wearing a—"

His eyes shifted from the grunt to Lou and her father, and his jaw dropped open. He mumbled something and grappled with his shotgun, fumbling with it as he tried to raise it waist high.

David whipped around, drawing a semi-automatic, and pulled the trigger twice. Twin shots hit the man in his chest and he lurched backward. The shocked expression on his face frozen into place, he fell against the door frame and then onto the threshold, blood instantly spreading from underneath his body. The second he hit the floor, a posse of armed men appeared in the street.

Lou caught Sarah Jane by the shirt collar and yanked her off balance toward the hallway at the far end of the parlor. Her father turned and coldcocked the attending grunt in the face. The grunt's head snapped backward, his eyes rolled back, and he collapsed to the floor, crashing into the coffee table. It knocked the book into the air, and it skidded across the floor into Lou's path. With her free hand, she scooped it up and bounded into the hallway.

Halfway along the corridor, she pushed Sarah Jane to the floor behind her, unsnapped her chest strap, shrugged the pack to the floor, and turned to face the parlor. Her father had drawn a second handgun. He stood with his feet shoulder width apart, his focus on the cadre of Cartel regulars now advancing on the museum.

To his left was the housemother. She stood motionless for a moment and then reached down to the broken coffee table. She picked up one of the legs, which was splintered on one end, and gripped it with both hands. David didn't see her.

Lou plucked one of the blades from her hip and, taking two quick bounds forward, whipped the knife at the woman as she lunged toward her father with the sharp end of the table leg.

The knife zipped the short distance and flipped only half a revolution. It didn't travel exactly where Lou aimed it. She'd tried to hit the woman squarely in the meat of her shoulder. Instead, the blade arced and drilled the woman's right hand, nailing it to the table leg.

She screeched in pain and dropped to her knees two feet from David. With her free hand, she tried prying the knife from her hand. She wriggled it free and dropped the leg in favor of her injured hand. She rolled onto her back, wailing.

Her voice was audible for only a beat before the gunfire erupted in earnest. David fired shots from each of the pistols before he sought cover behind one of the chairs.

Lou looked over her shoulder at Sarah Jane. The girl was lying on her back on the floor, leaning on her elbows. Her face was paler than before, if that was possible, and her eyes were twice as large.

Lou crawled back to her and put her hand on Sarah Jane's bare foot. It was cold to the touch. "Stay here," she said, trying to speak over the prattle of the gunfire. "You'll be safe. Stay down. Stay here. My dad will take care of it."

Sarah Jane nodded hyperbolically. She curled her toes.

Lou let go and turned back to the fray. She used her elbows and knees to inch her way along the hall and into the parlor. Her father's Mossberg was on the floor, not far from the woman. It had fallen off the chair where her father had rested it. He was using another chair and a side table he'd flipped onto its side to protect him from the combination of small-arms fire and random shotgun blasts. His protection was holding for now, though not for long. There were three men at the doorway. None had managed to cross the threshold yet, but David only had so much ammunition in the two handguns. The .38 was in his back waistband, but she couldn't remember if he'd reloaded it on their way to the museum.

As the woman wailed in pain, her scowl now more a grotesque exaggeration of the frown she'd proudly worn before, Lou sensed she had a split second to snag the Mossberg and help her father.

Staying low, she resumed her commando crawl across the floor. The rug bunched under her stomach as she neared the rifle. Elbow. Knee. Elbow. Knee. She was almost there.

She was within arm's length of the rifle, no more than two feet from the pain-blind housemother, when she reached for the Mossberg. Her bruised ribs protested, but she extended her arm and hand as far as she could. Her outstretched fingers touched the butt of the rifle, and she inched her body forward enough to grip it. Before she could tug it toward her, however, the housemother rolled onto her side and locked her beady eyes on Lou. Then, with her bloody, injured hand, she gripped Lou's wrist and yanked her from the rifle. The woman then grabbed the weapon by its muzzle, its business end pointing at her chest. She scrambled on the floor, trying to gain real control of the rifle. Lou remembered her training and, instead of panicking, slowed her breathing and devised an instantaneous response.

She rose to her knees and leaped forward, like a cat, far enough to reach the Mossberg's ventilated handguard. She wrapped her tiny hand around it and pulled it close enough to find the trigger. The housemother yanked back, playing tug-of-war with the rifle, as Lou's fingers slipped inside the trigger guard and applied pressure.

The rifle kicked back toward her violently, slamming into her elbow, and a percussive thump boomed through her body. She closed her eyes at the blast, which was louder than the pops and smacks of gunfire coming from the front entrance.

When she opened them, the housemother lay on her side, her head resting on her outstretched arm. Her eyes were fixed open. Her mouth wasn't frowning anymore. Her jaw hung open, her bright pink tongue drooping from the side like an exhausted puppy.

There was a new stain on her smock. It was crimson and appeared to bloom across the fabric. The housemother was dead.

Lou yanked the rifle free from the dead woman's grip, held it to her chest, and rolled to her father. He was returning fire enough to keep the growing numbers of grunts at bay. They'd still not burst through the open door. They seemed content to use their overwhelming firepower to outlast her father from a distance before making their approach.

"Here!" she yelled to him over the din of a chorus of shotgun blasts. "Use this!"

He smiled at her and took the rifle. "Get out of here, Lou. I'm sure there's a way out back."

"No," she said and rolled away from him.

She was back at the housemother's body. Somehow the woman had more expression on her face in death than she had in life. Lou searched the rug with her hands until she found the black matte handle of her knife. She wiped it unceremoniously on the woman's dress and commando crawled backward toward the hall.

With the Mossberg in hand, her father was pinging grunts like they were targets in a shooting gallery. One after the other, he scored a hit, keeping the growing army at bay. From the relative safety of the hallway entrance, Lou watched her father practice what he'd preached to her. As she soaked in the gravity of the skirmish in which they'd found themselves, his words echoed in her head.

"I didn't say we couldn't do it. I said it wasn't easy and it could be dangerous."

He was right. Her father was pretty much always right. He'd proven it again and again. She wondered, then, why he hadn't insisted on taking her north of the wall against her wishes. Why, as her father, hadn't he demanded they work their way to Lawton, Oklahoma, and settle there? Surely, whatever the environment in Lawton had become, however it might have devolved, it couldn't be worse or more dangerous than San Angelo, Texas. It couldn't be more violent than the gun battle they were trying to escape from. It couldn't be.

A pair of bullets ripped past her head and exploded into the plaster wall. As a spray of debris showered over her, she understood why he'd brought her here, why he'd taken the more difficult of the two paths.

It wasn't only because she knew he sensed her deep need to somehow reconcile Scull Newman's death and that she wanted to, in some way, make good by delivering the ring. It was because of what he had told her in the moments after he'd set fire to her mother's and brother's remains in their backyard. The stinging odor of burnt gunpowder that filled the museum transformed into the sensory memory of the pyre that had consumed their bodies in pulsing flames and thick, billowing smoke.

"I won't always be here to protect you," he'd said to her as they stood in the garage. *"You need to learn to protect yourself."*

That was what he'd tried to help her do every day since. Knife throwing, hunting, fishing, camp building, martial arts, basic first-aid, love of books, and self-reliance in every sense of the word. The only thing he hadn't passed along was his knowledge of computers. That was superfluous in a world absent power.

"You have to grow up sooner than you should. You have to be ready to provide for yourself, to understand this is a dangerous world filled with dangerous people."

The dangerous people were at the door; they were dead or unconscious on the rug; they were in Archer City and in Austin. They were, as he'd told her, everywhere.

And so, she was certain, this trip into what he'd suspected might be a lion's den was an opportunity for him to test her skills. It was a calculated risk he'd taken to help her move past the emotional self-flagellation to which she'd ascribed after killing Scull Newman.

That was the only thing that made sense. She'd be sure to grill him about it once they made it out of San Angelo.

Lou turned to reach into her pack and find more ammo when Sarah Jane gripped her arm. Her cold fingers felt like ice against

Lou's adrenaline-heated skin.

"I know a way out," she said above the crack of the Mossberg, ducking reflexively even though she was flat against the floor. "Follow me."

Lou glanced past Sarah Jane. Other children peeked their heads out from their rooms, their hands gripping the molding of the door frames.

Lou stole a glance at her father and then locked eyes again with Sarah Jane. She tilted her head. Sarah repeated her call with more urgency. She cupped her hands around her mouth, and Lou noticed Sarah Jane had slipped her mother's wedding band onto her thumb.

"Hurry," she said. "I can help you."

Sarah Jane waved her hand, motioning for Lou to follow her. Lou held up a finger and turned back to her father. She retraced her crawl toward him and reached him as the first of the grunts breached the doorway.

She tugged on his pack, drawing it downward. "Dad! We need to go. Sarah Jane knows a way out."

Her father ignored her for a beat. He fired another shot, pivoted, and fired another. With the rifle still held against his shoulder and aiming toward the door, he looked at her. "What?" he called as a blast splintered the table and her father dropped to the floor next to her.

"Sarah Jane can lead us out of here. Let's go."

Without waiting for her father's response, she crawled backward toward the hallway. Her father glanced past her at Sarah Jane and followed her. He scurried past her and then dragged himself into the hall next to Sarah Jane.

He spun around and rose onto one knee to fire a series of defensive cover shots. "Go!" he yelled at the girls. "I'm right behind you."

Sarah Jane got to her feet, remaining hunched as she skittered away from the gunfire. Off balance, she bumped off the wall and nearly toppled over before catching herself with her hand. Lou followed her, slinging her backpack strap with one hand and scooping up the dog-eared book with the other.

She didn't see her father until she'd turned a corner, reached the end of a second hallway, and followed Sarah Jane through the last door on the right. He spilled into the room and shut the door behind them. Blood covered his shirt.

"Dad?" Lou screeched. She ran toward him, searching for the wound.

His face was already losing color. "I'm fine," he said, pushing her away. "It's no big deal. But we have to go. They'll be here in seconds."

Outside the room, the shooting had stopped. Lou could hear children crying. There was the sound of men shouting and heavy boots pounding against the solid wood floor. Sarah Jane had already opened the window leading to the alley beside the museum and flung open a closet door. She pushed aside the hanging clothes and removed a plaster-colored wooden panel from its wall, motioning for Lou and her father to climb into the two-by-two square hole.

There was a banging on the door from the hallway. Someone tried the locked handle. It jiggled as if it might give under the pressure. A voice yelled for Sarah Jane to let them in. She held her finger up to her lips and again motioned for Lou and her father to escape through the secret passage.

"This was for men trying to escape the law or their wives," said Sarah Jane, her face blushing in the dim light that filtered in through the open window. "It'll help you escape."

There was another loud bang against the door. Lou moved to the opening, tossed in her pack and the book, and hesitated. She touched Sarah Jane on the shoulder. "Why?" Lou asked.

"I don't care who you are," Sarah Jane said, "or what you did. The Cartel aren't good people. My dad wasn't a good man. I loved him, but he wasn't good. You seem good."

She gave Lou a thumbs-up. Lou thanked her and crawled into the hole, her father right behind her. She found her pack and the book, pushing them ahead of her in the narrow, dank passageway.

As soon as her father was inside, the tunnel went completely dark. Sarah Jane had covered the hole. Then Lou heard the closet door slide shut.

From behind them, Lou could hear the muffled sound of the door bursting open and Sarah Jane's voice telling the Cartel they'd escaped through the window.

"Keep moving," Lou's father whispered from behind her.

Lou hadn't even realized she'd stopped. She felt around her, trying to get a sense of her bearings, though she couldn't resolve anything other than she was crawling on hardened dirt. Although she hadn't noticed that at first, now she felt it under her palms and knees. The walls were dirt too, and the tunnel itself sloped downward. At one point the drop was relatively steep, and her pack slid ahead of her, scraping against the earthen floor.

"We need to stop," she said, whispering to her father. "You've been bleeding for too long."

"I'm fine," her father mumbled.

He wasn't fine. His breathing and the amplified sounds of him dragging his body through the tunnel indicated he needed help now. They couldn't wait any longer.

Lou wiggled her body onto her back and untied the knotted knife belt at her waist. She slid the sheathed knives free of the belt and tucked the blades into her waistband, one knife on each hip. Then she awkwardly twisted around in the two-foot-wide tunnel and sighed. "Where exactly are you hurt?"

"My arm," he whispered back. "I got grazed. Twice. I'll be okay. I need to clean it and wrap it once we're out of here."

"You need a tourniquet. Give me your arm."

Lou reached out and took his right hand. He guided her hand to the spot on his left arm just below the twin wounds. The blood was warm on his arm. It was pooling atop her fingers. It wasn't gushing, which was what would normally call for a tourniquet, but she couldn't risk him passing out. He guided her hand past the injury up to near his shoulder.

She took the knotted belt in her mouth and wound it around his arm above the bicep, looped it, and pulled on both ends. Her father growled in pain and she winced. Lou moved her fingers back to the spot where she'd felt the flowing blood. It had stopped.

"We'll keep this on until I can finish," she said. "But we can't leave it on there too long."

"Thank you." He exhaled loudly, puffing hot air from his cheeks. He sounded as though he'd been holding his breath for more than a minute while she applied pressure to stop the bleeding.

A chill ran along Lou's spine. It was colder here in the dark tunnel than it was outside or in the house, and the tunnel began to feel endless as she pushed along her pack. She set the book on top of it to make the progress easier.

She half expected the Cartel to give chase, but they didn't come. She and her father crawled slowly and as quietly as they could, until the pack hit something and she couldn't push it any farther. They'd reached the end of the tunnel. Lou shoved the pack as far as she could to one side and cozied up next to it. Her fingers groped the edges of the wall, searching for a ledge, a latch, a handle—anything she could grip. There wasn't anything discernible, so she inched against the wall and pressed her shoulder into it. Using her knees and thighs, she leaned into the wall and grunted, using all of her force to find an opening. It didn't give.

She scooted back from the wall. A sheen of cold sweat had matted her bangs to her forehead under her hat and chilled the back of her neck. She wiped both with her hand, then rubbed her hand on her thigh, which made her think of wiping the blood from her knife, which made her think of her father's injury.

"How are you?" she asked.

He touched her side. "I'm okay. Focus on getting us out of here. Don't worry about me."

"I tried pushing it and pulling it," said Lou. "It won't move. Can you try?"

"I can't get past you. There's not enough room. There's nothing there to grip?"

Lou shook her head even though she knew he couldn't see her. She couldn't see the tip of her own nose. "No," she whispered. "I know we're at the end, but it won't move."

"Did we miss a turn somewhere?"

"I don't think so. I felt the walls on both sides the whole way."

They sat there in the cold darkness for another minute. Lou shivered. Despite having stopped the bleeding, she knew her father was in pain, and it wasn't good to leave the tourniquet on for long. They didn't have much time to figure out a way out of the tunnel. They couldn't go all the way back. Chances were, the Cartel grunts were still in the museum and swarming around the front and side of it. It was possible that escaping the tunnel would only serve to put them right into the middle of a collection of armed, vengeful grunts.

"What about above you?" asked her dad.

It was an obvious, but overlooked possibility. She had tried every other option. Lou slowly reached above her head. The ceiling of the tunnel was a mixture of dirt and random planks of hewn pine. As she ran her fingers along it, a sprinkle of the packed soil dusted her head. Some of it got into her mouth, and she spat it out with a loud raspberry sound. Then she froze, remembering where they were and how important it was to be quiet.

There was no indication anyone other than her father had heard her. She raised her hands again and groped the ceiling for an opening. She ran her fingers toward her father and then back again to the end of the tunnel. That was where she found it. Mixed in with the dirt was a small metal ring. Lou slid her fingers inside it and pulled. It didn't budge.

Still holding the ring perpendicular to the ceiling, she raised her body and used the back of her neck and her shoulders to push. It didn't take much effort. Another shower of dirt rained onto her, but the ceiling creaked upward on a hinge.

The trapdoor was four feet long but only eighteen inches wide. Lou hadn't felt it because it didn't extend all the way to the sidewalls and it wasn't flush with the end of the tunnel.

She flung the door open and it slammed against the floor above them with a loud, resonant thud. Lou winced at the noise and looked into the dark abyss above them.

"Where does it lead?" asked her father.

"I can't tell," said Lou, blinking away the remnants of dirt still filtering through the air. "It's too dark."

Her father rustled against the floor and then tapped her side with something cold. Lou reached blindly for it and took it in her hand, recognizing it as his flashlight. She felt for the top end of it, aimed it through the opening, and pressed the power button with a loud click. Nothing happened.

"Shake it."

Lou shook the flashlight and tried again. The familiar bright white LED beam shone through the opening. "We could have used this earlier."

"I guess. I didn't think about it. I was too busy trying to avoid getting shot for the third time."

Lou thought better than to argue with a wounded man who'd been shot twice trying to protect her. She centered herself beneath the rectangular egress and stood up slowly to poke her head into the space above the tunnel.

Carefully, flinching because she expected to hit her head on something as she rose, she peered above the opening and then squeezed her arm through to illuminate her surroundings.

The dust particles floating in the air and reflecting the beam of light were so distracting, Lou couldn't focus on what lay beyond.

Once she recognized what it was that clouded her vision, she was able to better decipher where the tunnel had led them.

The room had a distinct, sweet odor despite the heavy layers of dust that appeared to cling to everything. Lou vaguely recognized the scent, but she couldn't place it.

The space wasn't large. Lou figured it was fifteen feet square. Lining the walls were floor-to-ceiling wooden barrels. They were labeled with markings, but Lou couldn't read them. Other than the barrels and a single wooden chair, the room was empty. Straight above her, wire-framed circular lamps were hanging from the ceiling. They were crisscrossed with spiderwebs that seemed to vibrate.

She lowered her head back into the tunnel and turned off the flashlight. It was better to be in the dark than shine the light on her dad and see something she didn't want to see. The sight of him bleeding as he entered Sarah Jane's bedroom was enough.

"It's empty, whatever it is," she said. "It's not big, but it has barrels along the walls."

"Wooden barrels?"

"Yes," she replied.

"Whiskey," David said. "I thought I smelled it."

"Whiskey, like alcohol?"

"Exactly like alcohol. C'mon, let's climb up there and figure out how to blow this joint."

Lou picked up her pack, unzipped it, and stuffed the book inside. She couldn't close the top of the pack completely because it was so full, but she did her best and heaved the bag over her head and onto the floor of the room above them.

"Hand me your pack, Dad."

David protested, then relented and handed it over. She took it with both hands and shoved it up and through the opening at an angle. It crashed with a thud above them, shaking free more of the dirt that hung from the tunnel's ceiling.

Lou then climbed through the hole herself, standing first, then using her arms to lift herself onto the floor as she might have climbed from the edge of a swimming pool onto the deck. Once safely in the room, she plucked the flashlight from her pocket and shone it through the hole toward her father. He hadn't yet emerged from the tunnel, so the light wasn't in his eyes or, thankfully for Lou, on his wounds.

"Hand up the rifle," she said. "Then you only have to worry about yourself."

Lou heard a series of clicks, and then the butt of the rifle appeared at the opening, absent its magazine. She reached down and pulled up the Mossberg, setting it on the wooden floor next to her, a plume of dust rising to meet her face. She sneezed.

"God bless you," David said. "Scoot back and give me some room."

She did, averting the light, and David grunted his way from the tunnel into the storage room. Once he'd finished the push onto the floor, he collapsed next to Lou and sighed.

"Quite a day, huh?" he asked her. "All for a ring. I feel a little bit like Frodo Baggins."

"Who?" asked Lou.

"Frodo," David said through labored breaths. "He was a character in a series of books by J. R. R. Tolkien. He was a hobbit."

"A hobbit?"

"Like a human, but smaller. With hairy feet."

"What were the books?"

"There was a trilogy called *The Lord of the Rings*," he said. "And a related book called *The Hobbit*."

"Frodo was in all of them?"

"No," said her father. "He was in *The Lord of the Rings*. His relative Bilbo was in *The Hobbit*."

"Did Frodo get shot?"

David grunted. "No. Not really."

"Then we can talk about him later," said Lou. "We need to get you fixed first."

Her father chuckled weakly. "Let's find a way out."

Lou shook the flashlight again and clicked on the LED beam. She scanned the room, passing the barrels. She could now tell they read *Rebecca Creek*. There was a faint star in the middle of a circle above the name, which also proclaimed to be *Fine Texas Spirit Whiskey*.

Lou found a barricaded door along the wall to her left. There was a long wooden plank set across the door's midsection. She crossed the room, keeping the beam aimed at the barricade. Her boots clopped on the floor, which creaked and moaned under her slight weight. She put the flashlight in her mouth, bit down on it to hold it, and reached for the barricade.

Her father met her at the door, and together they lifted the wooden plank and dropped it to the floor. It sent a cloud of dust into the air around them, and Lou sneezed again. Her father coughed.

"Let me go first," he said.

Lou aimed the light at the door and found a large wooden handle screwed into the door on its left side. Her father gripped the handle and slowly pulled it inward. A tall bead of light expanded into the whiskey room as he cracked the door farther open and peered outside.

Lou clicked off the flashlight and stuffed it in her pocket. She stepped away from the door, giving her father room, and he stuck his head through the opening. She glanced at his arm and saw his shirt soaked with blood. It had run along his arm and stained the side of his pants too. At least she'd quelled the bleeding for the time being. That was a plus, sort of.

His hand trembled as he held it alongside the door. Lou swallowed hard. She wondered if his pale skin was filtered through the bright light from the outside or if he'd actually lost color.

She averted her eyes from the injury as he slipped back inside. He closed the door until a sliver of floor-to-ceiling light filled the thin gap between the frame and edge of the door. It creaked as he moved it, the hinges as dust-filled as the rest of the forgotten space.

"We're on the opposite side of the street from the back of the museum," he said. "There's nobody around, but I think we need to wait here until nightfall to leave. We can't risk going now."

Lou sighed. A mix of relief and fear settled in her gut. She was glad they were not going now, not so excited about the prospect of waiting around for another few hours. Her father needed help now.

"Okay," she said, retrieving the flashlight from her pocket. "I guess I need to fix you up in the dark."

He let the door close and sighed.

Lou crossed the room and found the lone chair. She dragged it across the floor, not as worried about making noise now, and patted the seat with her hand. Dust bloomed above the chair and she swatted it away. "Have a seat," she said, doing her best impression of a nurse. "This will only hurt a little."

She guided him to the chair with the LED beam, then left him in the dark as she turned to close the trapdoor and retrieve her pack. She dragged it back to the chair and knelt down, wiggled a finger in the gap at the top of the zipper, and yanked open the pack. She withdrew the heavy book and set it on the floor.

"What's that?" asked David.

"A book."

"Thanks. Which book?"

"The woman in there was reading it," she said. "I figured I'd take it."

Her father bent over and picked up the book. "Shine the light over here."

She grumbled and stopped rifling through her pack long enough to aim the beam at the book. Her father wiped the cover with his hand and then turned the book on its side to look at the spine. "*Lolita*," he said, "by Vladimir Nabokov. A little risqué for you, Lou."

She blindly felt around the inside of the pack with one hand, trying to locate a molded rectangular plastic box. With the other she held the light on the book. Her father opened the book, cracking its spine, and leafed backward to the title page. "Huh. This is the property of the Killeen Public Library."

"She probably owes a lot of late fees, then," joked Lou. She found the box and jimmied it from the pack. "I need the light now."

She aimed the LED beam at the white box marked FIRST AID. The lettering and the red cross in the middle of the box's lid were scratched and faded to an orange color. Using her thumb, she unlatched the twin catches on the lid and opened the box. Before pulling anything out of the kit, she glanced at her father. "No broken bones, right?"

"No," he said.

"Okay. No bullets or pieces of bullets?"

"I don't think so, but you'll have to look."

A wave of nausea washed through her body. She didn't like the idea of having to perform surgery on her father. She reached into the kit and removed a pair of surgical scissors.

"Are those sterile?" her father asked.

Lou shrugged. "I don't know."

"Getting an infection would be worse than the injury. You've got to sterilize everything you touch me with, got it?"

He sounded impatient, his words clipped. His tone was direct and without his usual soft compassion.

Lou understood he didn't mean to be rude or hurtful. He was in pain. His face was drenched with sweat. He'd lost the white hat somewhere in the tunnel, and his hair was matted flat against his brow and the tops of his ears.

Lou had isopropyl pads in the kit, but she wasn't sure that would be enough to cleanse all of the tools and, since she didn't have any Betadine or bleach handy, she'd need the pads to help clean the wound. She bit the inside of her cheek and stared into the dark corners of the room. Then it came to her.

Two birds. One stone.

She took a collapsible plastic cup from inside the kit and stood. With the flashlight in her hand, she hurried to the back wall of the room. She aimed the light at the top of one of the whiskey barrels standing on its end. Lou felt around the top of the lid for some sort of opening mechanism. She didn't find anything, so she ran the light along the side of the barrel until she saw a round wooden stopper protruding from the center of its face.

She didn't know the stopper was called a bung, she merely understood removing it would be the easiest way to access the barrel's contents. She gripped the edges of it with her finger but couldn't get enough leverage.

"What are you doing?" called her father.

"Sterilizing the tools," she called back.

She put a hand on her hip, considering the best way to open the bung. She ran her finger along the black matte handle of her knife, and another epiphany struck her. Lou drew the blade, dropped to one knee, and stabbed the knife into the center of the bung. She shimmied it halfway to the hilt and then turned it clockwise. It gave a bit, turning with the torque she applied. She turned it counterclockwise, and the bung loosened again.

Back and forth she turned the handle, bruising the pads on her palms. But it worked. One final counterclockwise twist freed the bung with a pop. A gush of whiskey poured from the barrel, drenching her legs and feet.

The pungent, sweet odor almost overwhelmed her, stinging her nostrils and the back of her throat. She held her breath and expanded the collapsible cup, held it under the open spout, and filled it with the golden-colored liquid.

She walked back to her father, holding the cup out in front of her as if it were a dirty diaper, and handed it to him. He took the cup. She shone her light on it.

"Drink up," she said. "It'll help with the pain."

"You remember that?" he asked, his voice full of surprise. "I didn't think you were listening."

She smirked. "I always listen. You explained how alcohol is a downer. It makes you sleepy and do stupid things. It also makes it easier to handle pain."

"Good girl," he said and toasted her as he swigged the cup. He grimaced. "Whew. That's strong."

Lou swept the light to her first aid kit. She collected every piece of surgical gear she could carry and then took the cup from her father on the way back to the barrel, where whiskey was still pulsing from the opening.

She filled the cup again and then held the tools under the whiskey waterfall, sterilizing the blades and needles. She tried holding her breath. Feeling a little light-headed from the intense fumes, she backed away.

"All right," she said, returning to her father. "Here we go. Hold this."

She handed him the flashlight, which he kept aimed at the area where she'd tied the belt around his arm. She loosened the knot at the center of the tourniquet and took it off. Carefully, she used the surgical scissors to cut free his sleeve. She cut all the way around his arm and then pulled the fabric down and over his hand.

She still couldn't see the depth of the wounds. There was too much blood. At least it wasn't flowing freely now.

"Okay," she said. "This is going to sting."

Her father nodded and sucked in a deep breath. He held it as she poured the cup of whiskey over his arm. He grunted, gritting his teeth and squeezing his eyes shut to fight the burn.

Lou ripped open a packet with an isopropyl-drenched towelette, unfolded it, and cleaned around the torn flesh on the outside of his bicep. Both wounds were remarkably close to one another, the second appearing to have ripped more widely open the first.

Tears streamed down her cheeks as she worked to slow her pulse and keep her breathing even. Each time her father flinched, she did too. Stinging bile crept up her throat. He was having trouble holding the light on the wound. She was guessing as she dabbed and wiped. A couple of times she hit a gash dead center and her father's body tensed and shuddered against her touch. She couldn't stand the thought of anything hurting her father, let alone her own hands. What came next would be the worst of all.

She'd decided the wound was clean enough that she could close it. If she hadn't been able to irrigate it enough, she'd have had to leave it open and pack it. That would have been the better option to prevent a bacterial infection. But since she'd managed to use the whiskey and the rubbing alcohol and hadn't found any bullet fragments, her father agreed with her that the better option was to close it.

Lou found a long rectangular package in the kit and tore it open, a disposable sterile drape. It was tacky around its edges, and she stuck it to her father's wounded arm, placing the fenestrated cloth such that the twin gashes were visible through the window.

It was one thing to practice stitches on the skin of dead animals, quite another to suture living human flesh. It would be softer and more pliable than that of dead tissue. At least that was what her father had told her. There was nothing better to perfect stitching up a wound than stitching up a wound.

Rivulets of sweat repopulated on her face and neck. Her hands were clammy. She'd rather have been sewing up herself.

Lou found a pair of powdered rubber gloves in the kit, blew into them as her father had taught her to do, and slipped them onto her hands. They were too big, so she had to work the excess material into the spaces between her fingers. She flexed her hands. The gloves weren't a great fit, but they'd have to do.

"Can you hold the light still?"

He nodded. "I think so."

"Okay," she said. "Here goes."

Lou squeezed the first of the tears on the outside of his bicep and temporarily closed the wound. The jagged edges didn't match exactly, but like the gloves, they were close enough.

Lou wished they had suture glue. It would have been faster, easier, and a lot less painful. She was stuck with an old-fashioned, half-moon size twelve suture needle. She opened the package and pulled out the pre-threaded needle. She exhaled and, with as steady a hand as she could manage, began sewing shut the first of the wounds.

Ten minutes and two needles later, she was finished. She'd managed the last couple of stitches without light. Her father was too exhausted to hold the LED beam steady enough to help.

When she was finished, she covered the wounds in raw honey, a better antibacterial than ointment, and then used pads and medical tape to cover it. She sank to her knees, exhausted, and lay back on the dusty floor.

Her father thanked her. He told her how much he loved her. He was proud of her, he said, not only for fixing him up, but for staying calm enough to do it. She didn't tell him she was falling apart on the inside. He was still talking to her when sleep took hold. Despite the cold, the dust, and the hard floor onto which whiskey had leeched, she was unconscious within minutes.

It was somewhere between midnight and three in the morning when her father woke her up, told her to get her pack, and follow him outside. They were going to Killeen, he said, and the sooner they left, the better.

CHAPTER 13

Lou dragged her boots across the dirt. She was shuffling along the shoulder of the crumbling highway, kicking up the mixture of dry earth and chunks of asphalt. It crunched under her boots like she was stomping on freshly poured gravel. It was warmer than it had been in days, the humidity was low, and it didn't feel like November. They were mostly through Mercury, a speck of a town smack-dab between San Angelo and Waco.

"I'm guessing they named it Mercury because it's like another planet," said Lou.

David finished taking a swig of water. At Lou's insistence, he'd been drinking more than his usual share since his injury.

"It's so small here it reads 'Now Leaving Mercury' on both sides of the sign," he said.

Lou started to ask if he was joking, but recognized the impish grin on his face before she bit. She reached for the canteen and he handed it to her. She shook it and then took a reserved sip.

They were halfway through their third full day on the road. They'd gone more than eighty miles east since leaving San Angelo. Aside from a boy playing with an injured bird along the side of the highway outside Doole, they hadn't seen another soul along the way.

It was a meandering, dusty path that led them toward Killeen. And while they'd walked through countless small towns, Mercury was unique in its lack of size. There was the Baptist church, which they now passed as they turned south for a short distance before heading east again, and virtually nothing else.

"We could stop here if you want," David said. "It might be alien, but it's pretty here. I'm guessing there's nobody to bother us. Ever."

His mood and color had improved greatly over the past couple of days. The travel was much slower than their usual pace. Lou had indulged him and, in fact, enjoyed not having to keep pace with his normally long strides.

After a night's sleep and a good, bountiful meal of possum and squirrel, he'd started to come around. The wounds were healing. He'd praised her craftsmanship every time they changed the dressing. The stitches would leave scars, but the wounds were healing cleanly and, so far, they'd avoided infection. Copious amounts of raw honey were doing the trick.

Lou kicked a larger chuck of asphalt and watched it tumble ahead of her before bouncing into the air and skittering on the road. There were veins of excess tar that spread out across the two-lane highway.

She scanned one side of the road and then the other, eyeing a couple of large properties with decent-looking houses. Nothing, though, had her excited about the prospect of staying in Mercury. She'd rather keep walking.

"I'm fine with Killeen," she answered. "I like the idea of living in a library."

"I thought you would," said David. "I like the prospect too. An endless supply of books is never a bad thing. You can learn a lot while we're there."

Lou had given a lot of thought to the idea of living in a library. It was comforting and would provide for a constant escape from reality.

It could be an oasis in the middle of a desert, a place where she could learn about the world without having to venture into it.

They turned east, leaving Mercury, and Lou stepped back up onto the road. It was in better condition than it had been for miles and made it easier to traverse. She imagined there were plenty of books in the library about travels, about daughters and their fathers, about a world gone to pot.

"What's your favorite book?" she asked her dad. "What book could you read again and again?"

"That's complicated."

Lou stopped and lifted a boot, plucking a piece of asphalt from her boot tread. "Why?"

"That's like asking me my favorite song. I have many. It depends on my mood or what mood I'd like to have."

"List them."

"The songs or the books?"

"The books," she said. "When we get to Killeen, I'm going to read all of them."

Her father checked his boots. They were clean. "That's ambitious."

"I'll have plenty of time, as long as Earlene doesn't show up and claim the library as her own."

David laughed. It was a true laugh that came from his core. Lou laughed too.

He sighed. "Well, let's see. I love biographies. A well-written biography is more entertaining than fiction, even if sometimes the biographers are prone to embellishment."

"I like biographies," said Lou.

"I like *The Art of War*. Its philosophy is applicable to so many different parts of life. It was written by the Chinese general and strategist Sun Tzu," he said. "It's an old book."

"So, it teaches you to fight?"

"Yes and no. One of the greatest bits of advice is that '*Supreme excellence consists of breaking the enemy's resistance without fighting.'"*

"That's hard to do," Lou said.

"Very."

The sun had inched past its zenith. It was a bright orange ball of gas in the sky. There weren't any clouds. Lou raked her teeth across her dry lips. They were cracked, and she reached up with a finger and picked at the loose skin until the coppery taste of blood seeped onto her tongue.

"I like *Frankenstein*," David said after they'd walked for a few minutes in silence. "It's a sad book but a good study of the human condition."

"Who wrote it?" Lou asked. "What's his name?"

Her father glanced at her, a sly grin creeping across his face. "*Her* name was Mary Shelley. She was British and lived in the eighteen hundreds. She wrote biographies and essays too. I think that's what made *Frankenstein* so good."

"What's it about?"

"You'll have to read it. Or I can read it to you. It's about a scientist who creates a monster from the body parts of dead people."

"Gross."

"That's the surface plot," said David. "It's really more about power and love and hubris. It's complicated."

"What else?"

"*The Godfather*. Mario Puzo wrote it. It's also about power and love and hubris and how the consuming desire for those things can ultimately destroy someone."

"Is there a monster in that book too?"

David squinted into the distance, considering her question before answering. "Yes, but not like Frankenstein's monster."

Lou rolled her tongue around in her cotton mouth, tasting the blood. She sucked on the floor of it, thinking about the books her father described. She wanted to read all of them. She wanted to lose herself in stories of power and love and hubris.

"What's hubris?" she asked.

"Self-destructive arrogance."

Yes. Power and love and hubris. The more books about those things she could find, the better.

CHAPTER 14

The Oveta Culp Hobby Memorial Library was the most beautiful building Lou had ever seen. It sat majestically on the Central Texas College campus. A Spanish tile roof framed a wall of windows that looked out over a sloping lawn and decorative pond.

A footbridge connected walking paths across a section of the pond and led directly to the library's entrance. An amorphous, struggling hedge, which appeared as though it had once been a trio of topiaries, and a handful of dying trees dotted the overgrown grassy lawn surrounding the property.

Lou's heart fluttered and she resisted the urge to run up the slope to the building's entrance. Despite her exhaustion from the last one hundred miles of the trek east, she was anxious to run her finger along the spines of books and pick the right one as her first escapist adventure.

Her father cautioned her to approach slowly. They didn't know yet if the building was occupied or easily accessible.

They'd successfully avoided two Cartel posses on their way into Killeen. Neither of the armed groups on horseback had seen the pair

146

as they sneaked their way to the campus. Since their deadly encounter in San Angelo, they'd managed a peaceful existence.

Lou still had trouble sleeping. Scull Newman haunted her uneasy dreams. So did the housemother, whose name Lou had never learned. She'd come to dread falling asleep, anticipating the inevitable nightmares that would follow.

This new place, the library, brought with it the promise of filling her head with so many fantasies that one of them was bound to replace the specter of the people she'd killed. At least she hoped that would happen.

The two of them warily approached the grand building. In truth, it was as run-down and in need of repair as any other place they'd come across since the Scourge. Neglect and Mother Nature had a way of turning even newer, solid constructions into hovels on the brink of collapse. But to Lou, the library was a beacon of hope and, as such, gleamed with incomparable beauty.

They crossed the last bit of the lawn, the knee-high weedy blades brushing against them, and found themselves in front of the bank of glass windows that made up most of the north-facing side of the building.

There were two pairs of narrow glass doors set into the wall of windows. David first tried the set on the left. They rattled, but didn't open. Neither did the other doors. Both pairs were locked. He took a step back and surveyed the facade.

"The good news is that I don't see any broken glass," David said. "That means it's unlikely anybody has ravaged the place. Perhaps we'll get lucky and find everything intact once we find a way inside."

Lou stepped close to the wall and spun her ball cap backward on her head. She pressed her face to the glass and cupped her hands around them. Her warm breath reflected off the glass in short blooms onto her face.

The building looked intact all right. It was marvelous.

A blue and yellow industrial carpet stretched the length and width of the floor, with an abstract pattern that reminded Lou of seashells awash in a tide. Sitting atop the carpet and evenly spaced were bookshelves of varying heights. Some, probably the children's section, were only three feet tall. Others, maybe replete with biographies or classic literature, were seven feet and stuffed with books.

The mahogany-colored bookshelves were too many to count. Sprinkled amongst them were tables and desk chairs. There were even comfy-looking loungers dotting the wide-open space. Her stomach fluttered and she sighed. They were so close.

"C'mon," said her dad. "Let's find another way inside."

Lou took one last sweeping look at the room and stepped away. She watched her breath evaporate on the glass and then turned away to follow her father around the eastern side of the building.

They stepped to another opening, one that was recessed into an alcove. It too was locked, so they bounded down a short set of concrete steps and into the high grass to find a way around the side of the building. The grass thinned as they worked their way along the eastern edge, hugging the brick facade. They were on dirt now. The earth was solid and veined with cracks from the prolonged lack of rain. Lou thought the ground looked like her lips felt, and she ran a finger along them.

They reached a covered walkway with a collapsing aluminum roof and rusting support poles. Paint peeled and flaked from the poles, revealing previous layers of color underneath the top coat. Lou's dad helped her over a waist-high railing that bordered the covered path on both sides. When they jumped the second railing, they were in a stone-tiled courtyard that served as a centerpiece for the library and several other campus buildings. The joints in the tile were overrun with weeds, and an octagonal fountain at the center of the courtyard was dry, its centerpiece broken, and the adornment at its top, whatever it had once been, was missing. There were four planters surrounding the dry fountain. There were thick, knee-high stumps in each of the planters and the remnants of fluorescent orange spray-paint markings cut off at the sawed top of the stumps.

Lou imagined students had once studied here. The trees might have provided shade under which to sit and read or write. The bubbling fountain and its cascading water would have proved calming. The rectangular stone tiles were likely smart and clean, giving the courtyard a modern appearance. She was daydreaming about the space's past when her father called out to her. He was standing near the southern side of the library. There were eight arches that led into a pedestrian porte cochère. Four sets of steps led through the arches.

"Lou, I think I found a way inside."

She bounded across the stone tiles, her pack bouncing against her back as she bounded up the steps and into the darker, partially enclosed rear entrance. It took a moment for her eyes to adjust, but when they did, she saw her dad standing at the far end of the space. His hands were on his hips, and he was studying a piece of weathered plywood affixed to the building about eight feet above the ground.

Lou walked over, her thumbs tucked inside her pack straps. "What's that?"

"I'm pretty sure it's where they used to have a wall-mounted air-conditioning unit. I think I can put you on my shoulders and help you climb inside once we've pried off the wooden board."

Lou unsnapped her chest strap and shrugged off the pack, dropping it to the ground. She took off her hat and ran her fingers through her hair before replacing the hat. She worked the bill, rounding its shape with her fingers.

Her father smiled. "I take it you agree?"

"Sure. I want to get inside."

He took off his own pack. "Let's get the board free. You climb through, then unlock a door from the inside."

Lou nodded and stepped into her father's laced hands. He hoisted her onto his shoulders, held her knees with his hands, and moved her close to the thin plywood board. She ran her fingers at the corners, across the heads of black wood screws. They had a touch of rust on the edges of the heads. She wiggled her fingers in the narrow gap between the back side of the board and the wall.

"You okay?" David asked, readjusting his hold on her legs.

"Yes," she grunted, pulling on the board.

Despite how thin the board was, it didn't give. She tugged again. There was no way to get enough leverage between the board and the wall.

She balled her hands into fists and flexed her fingers. Her knuckles were stiff. She tried again by pulling from the corners at the top and then at the bottom. No luck. Lou grunted with frustration and balled her hands into fists again. This time, though, she reared back and punched the center of the board. Her momentum knocked her father off balance and he swayed backward.

"Whoa," he said, regaining his footing. "Be careful."

"Sorry," Lou said, putting a hand on his head. She patted it in apology. "I think I figured out something."

"What?"

She put her hand up to the center of the board and pushed inward. The board gave with the pressure, bending in toward the hole it covered. When she did that, the corners bowed away from the wall, providing a sliver more room.

"I think I can get it," she said. "But I have to try something else."

"Okay, but let me know if you're going to go all crazy on me again."

Lou pulled a blade from her hip. "Could you get closer to the wall, please?"

Her father inched closer. He wrapped his arms around her lower legs and clasped his hands together, locking his hold.

With her left shoulder, Lou leaned into the center of the board and felt it give. Then she reached up with her right hand and slid the blade between the corner of the board and the wall. Thinking the thin beginnings of rust had compromised the screw's integrity, she sawed the blade until she felt it give.

"Got it!" she said excitedly. "I got it!"

"Great. Now what?"

Lou stuck the blade back against her hip and reached up to the freed corner with both hands. She wrapped her fingers around the edges and pulled diagonally downward.

"Back up, Dad. Close your eyes in case it snaps."

David backed away, one solid step at a time, and Lou kept hold of the board. First the screw on the upper left snapped. Then the bottom screws gave simultaneously, and Lou dropped the board to the ground.

David patted her shin. "Good job. Now for the fun part."

He walked Lou back to the wall. The opening wasn't completely open. There was a messy wad of pink fiberglass insulation stuffed into the rectangular hole.

"Be careful with that," David said, craning his neck to try to see what she was doing. "Don't get it in your eyes."

Lou carefully plucked the wad free of the hole and dropped it to the ground next to the wood board. She wasn't finished yet. There was another board plugging the hole on the opposite side of the opening, but this board was easier to pry free.

She ducked into the opening and, using all of her weight, pushed on the board. It took a couple of attempts, but it popped off in one piece and tumbled into the library. Lou caught a whiff of the interior, and a smile spread across her face. She inhaled deeply, soaking in the aroma of books. There was a musty, comforting odor filtering through the hole.

She patted her father's head. "I need to turn around. I've got to go legs first."

Her father spun around so his back was against the wall. He let go of her legs, and Lou pressed her back against the brick and awkwardly climbed upward on his shoulders. He reached up and balanced her by steadying her calves.

She raised one leg and bent forward, mimicking the arabesque ballet position she'd learned in gymnastics. She guided her foot into the hole and rested it there while she braced herself by pressing her hands onto her father's shoulders. Certain she had her balance, she raised her second leg and slid that foot into the hole. She pushed up and slid her legs farther into the opening.

David reached up with his hands over his head, his back still to the wall, and Lou took them one at a time. Then he extended his arms upward, lifting her high enough that her torso slipped into the opening.

"I'm good," she told him, and he let go.

She wiggled herself backward, the narrow opening digging into her abdomen, and grabbed the brick on the outside wall where it met the bottom edge of the hole. Her legs now dangled free inside the library. Using every bit of strength remaining, she eased herself backward until she was hanging flat against the interior drywall, her feet less than four feet from the floor. She let go and dropped, landing awkwardly and tumbling backward.

She caught herself with her hands and stopped the back of her head from hitting the carpeted floor. Her back ached, and her stomach muscles burned, but she'd done it.

Ignoring the minor pain that radiated from the small of her back, she jumped to her feet and skipped to the doors. There was a large latched deadbolt on each of them. She picked one, turned it, and swung open a heavy, steel-frame glass door. She started to run out to get her pack when her father held up his hand. "Wait! Keep the door open. We don't know if it'll lock automatically when it closes."

Lou curbed her momentum and stayed at the door, holding it for him as he approached. He put his hand on her head, atop her cap, and then ran his fingers down to her cheek before pinching it.

"Good job, Lou. Well done."

An involuntary smile broadened across her face. "Thanks, Dad. I can't wait to start reading."

"Let me get the packs; then we'll take a tour of the place. We need to make sure we can stay here. After that we have to clean up our mess and plug that hole. Then you can pick out some books."

Lou frowned. "It'll be dark by then. I won't be able to read."

"Then you'll wait until morning. First things first."

Lou begrudgingly agreed and leaned against the open door while her father retrieved their packs. He set them on a round table closest to the door. Then he picked up the splintered pieces of the thin plywood board and the clumps of insulation, bringing them inside.

"No need to let any passersby know we're here," he said with a wink.

Lou closed the door behind him and turned the lock. She exhaled and surveyed the room. It was the first good look she gotten since peeking through the window on the opposite side of the building. The first thing that struck her was the dust. It was everywhere, like a thin layer of snow or ash. That was a good sign nobody had been here for a long time. She stepped to the table where her father had set the packs and dragged a finger along the lacquered wood, leaving a clean path where her finger had been.

David had moved a chair over to the opening through which she'd crawled and was working to reaffix the board against the drywall. He was mumbling to himself with the board overhead.

"I thought we were taking a tour first?" she asked.

He grunted and slapped the board against the wall. "I changed my mind. Better to secure the place first. Then we don't have to worry about anything while we're exploring."

Lou looked longingly at the bookshelves around her. That was what *she* wanted to explore. "That makes sense."

He motioned to the floor with his chin. "Could you please hand me one of the screws? I know the holes are stripped, but I'm hoping I can still get the board to stick."

Lou handed him the screws one at a time, and he managed to

wiggle them into place. It took him some time, and a few false starts, but he got the board to hang. It covered the opening as it had before they'd arrived.

He hopped down from the chair and dusted off his hands. "Whew. This place needs a thorough cleaning, doesn't it? I think my allergies are going to go nuts."

"What now?" Lou asked.

"Let's explore."

The library was every bit as wonderful as Lou had imagined it would be. It was also every bit as utilitarian as her father had hoped.

In addition to the seemingly wide selection of books, the library had plenty of comfortable chairs. The carpeted floor was well padded and felt spring-like after having spent so much time treading on asphalt, concrete, and drought-packed dirt.

There was a staff break room that had a supply of canned food in a cabinet above the sink, a refrigerator, a microwave, and a coffee maker. Incredibly, all of it worked.

They discovered the power functioned, at least sporadically, when Lou flipped a switch on the wall at the entrance to the break room. Overhead fluorescent lights clinked and flickered to life. The refrigerator chugged and rumbled as it restarted. The microwave clocked flashed a reminder to reset the clock. The coffee maker beeped, and a pleasant-sounding female voice asked if they'd like to brew a small cup, a medium, or a large.

Lou and her dad locked eyes. Both of them grinned. They'd found their oasis indeed. Not only was there power, refrigeration, and a short supply of food, there was also running water.

They'd discovered functioning bathrooms, whose overhead lights illuminated whenever they entered them. Somehow, there was still cold water flowing from the sinks and recirculating in the toilets.

David hypothesized that there wasn't a supply of water, but rather reserve tanks. They'd have to conserve it as much as possible.

As for the power, it took them only an hour to discover it was coming from a bank of solar cells mounted on the library's roof. They'd found a control panel in the library director's office, mounted to the wall next to the electronic thermostat. The thermostat was on, but the system was off. David concluded there was enough power to run the lights and the appliances but not the air-conditioning or the heater. Not that they would have used them anyhow. The solar panel control module displayed real-time information on power consumption, the charge being generated by the solar cells, how much excess power one could sell back to the grid, or if the system was running at a deficit.

"I don't think we'll be selling anything back to the grid," said David, "given there *is* no grid anymore."

"Can we stay here?" Lou asked. "Please?"

"For now. As long as it's safe, we can stay. I don't know how long that will be. It could be a day. It could be a month. It could be—"

"Forever?"

Lou searched her father's eyes for something more than a noncommittal maybe. She understood the precarious, unpredictable nature of their world, but she still wanted her father to let her pretend everything was better now. She wanted to pretend she had a home again.

"Lou," he said softly, "I've told you before I'm only going to shoot straight with you. It doesn't do either of us any good for me to lie to you or make you believe something that isn't true."

Her shoulders drooped and she looked at the floor. "I know."

He touched her chin and lifted her head until her eyes met his. "I wish I could make everything better," he said, rubbing his thumb on her chin. "I wish I could bring back Mom and Davey. I wish I could erase all the bad that's happened. But I can't. I won't ever be able to do that. The best I can do is keep you safe."

"I know."

He sighed and narrowed his gaze. "Tell you what," he said after a few seconds of silence. "Let's call this place home, okay? This is our home. We're not going anywhere unless we're forced out. We're staying."

A warm, consuming sense of relief spread through her body. "Really?"

"Really. I don't see any reason to leave a place that has power, a refrigerator, and a microwave."

"And toilets," said Lou. "Don't forget about toilets."

"Of course." David chuckled. "Who could forget about toilets?"

"And toilet paper. Leaves suck."

"They do suck."

He smiled at her. "I love you, Lou. I want you to be happy. I want you to read as many books as you can plow through."

Lou threw herself against her father and wrapped her arms around his back. "Thank you. Thank you."

CHAPTER 15

Lou ran her fingers along the books like a kid rattling fence pickets with a stick. She was pretty certain she'd read every one of the books on the shelf, but wanted to be sure. Her stomach was full of squirrel, and the library was relatively warm despite the chill outside.

Like so many of the seven hundred plus days they'd lived in the library, this one was enjoyably unremarkable. Somehow, they'd avoided the Cartel attacks many others endured. Maybe it was the books, she'd joked with her dad. Intellect was a repellant for them.

She'd read close to a thousand books since they'd settled into what had become their home. On a good day she could devour three of them before bedtime, when her father would read to her until she drifted off to a comfortable sleep. The nightmares had been replaced with Arthurian adventures, visits to Narnia, Oceania, and travels aboard the *Pequod*.

She awoke each morning eager to dive back into the story she'd left unfinished the night before or crack open a new one. Her father would stack books on his favorite table, put his feet on the desk's edge, his legs crossed, and leaf through one book after another. He'd already read most of them, but told Lou a good book was like an old friend; it was always good to visit and catch up after time apart.

Today, she was going to start Sun Tzu's *The Art of War*. Her father had wanted her to read Machiavelli's Socratic dialogue of the same name. Then he'd suggested she read *The Prince*. She'd just completed it that morning. Now it was time for Sun Tzu and his version of Ping-fa, *The Art of War*.

She walked over to her father, her feet shuffling against the nap of the carpet, confident there weren't any other books she'd forgotten to put ahead of the ancient Chinese text. She pulled out the chair across from her dad and lifted her feet onto the table, crossing her legs and mimicking his posture.

"I'm ready for Sun Tzu," she said.

Her father, who was engrossed in Tolstoy's *War and Peace*, lifted his eyes above the top of the book and smiled.

Lou couldn't actually see his smile, but his eyes gave it away. She smiled back.

He lowered the book and closed it, holding a finger in place to mark his spot. He rubbed his eyes with the knuckles of his other hand and nodded. "You think so?"

"Yes. I've read Machiavelli."

"And?"

"And he's full of himself."

That drew a belly laugh from her father. "Why do you say that?"

Lou shrugged. "He thinks he knows what's best for the entire republic. That the key to a happy civilization is a strong army. Without the army, the other things can't survive."

Her father narrowed his eyes and pulled Tolstoy onto his lap. "What other things?"

"The rich, the poor, the public good."

"Is he wrong?"

She shrugged again and took off her cap. She ran her hands through her hair. They'd been using pond water to bathe. It wasn't the best, but it kept them clean, and Lou's hair was as healthy as it had been since the Scourge.

"I don't know," she said. "But it seems to me like...like..."

"Like what?"

"What's the word for the stuff that people in power want you to believe?" she asked, speaking with her hands. "They make it out to be fact, but maybe it's not?"

Her father pursed his lips. His chin wrinkled as he watched her struggle for the word.

"It's on the tip of my tongue," she said. "Like war movies. That sort of thing. Things that help patriotism."

Her father's expression relaxed. "Propaganda?"

She snapped her fingers and pointed at him. "Yes. Propaganda. The book, all seven chapters of it, sounds like propaganda."

"How so?"

"If you tell everybody the best way to keep them happy and safe is a big army, then they'll think they need a big army to be safe and happy."

"Huh," said David. He nodded with his eyes closed. "I hadn't thought of it that way. That's a cynical interpretation, isn't it?"

"Cynical?"

Lou sat there quietly for a moment, considering her reading of the five-hundred-year-old text. She didn't want to debate her father about Machiavelli's *Art of War*. She wanted to read Sun Tzu. The former was a means to an end so she could get to the latter. But David had made it a habit of discussing important books after she'd read them.

Agatha Christie and Sir Arthur Conan Doyle didn't get the same treatment as biographies, philosophical tomes, or the classics like Melville or Hemingway. For those, there was a cursory question or two. Clearly, Machiavelli warranted an inquisition.

Cynical.

How could she not be cynical? She was a child of the Scourge. Her government had abandoned her in favor of relinquishing it to a band of violent criminals. They'd done nothing to protect her or her father from the everyday dangers that grew from the vacuum the government had created when they'd built the wall so they could wash their hands of the mess that was Texas. It wasn't cynicism, it was realism. Maybe they were one and the same.

"I'm not saying you're wrong," said David. "That's very astute, actually. Given how Machiavelli wrote about power and manipulation, you very well might be right."

Lou eyed the prize on the table. Sun Tzu's thirteen-chapter masterpiece was atop one of the three stacks of books on the table. She leaned forward to snag it.

"Hold on," her father said gently. "Before you run off and start reading the book, I have some instructions for you."

Lou held her hand flat on the top of the book but didn't pick it up. She ran a finger across the gold foil lettering that spelled out the title.

"First I should tell you that Sun Tzu may or may not have existed. If he did, some scholars think he didn't write the book. It may be a compilation of the wisdom of many people."

"Okay," said Lou. "Why is that important?"

"You said that Machiavelli was arrogant, right? He thought he alone had all of the answers to a prosperous society under the thumb of strong, centralized rule."

"Right."

"With this book, it's not necessarily one person giving you the advice, it's many. That gives it more weight. That's why everyone from Napoleon, to Ho Chi Minh, to Colin Powell studied what is essentially a step-by-step instruction manual."

"Ho Chi who?"

"Vietnamese leader," David said. "Not that important."

"Got it. Anything else? You said 'first', so I figure there's more coming."

David smiled. "Consider whether or not this is a book about war at all. Or, rather, is it a book about peace?"

Lou scowled. "It's not called the *Art of Peace*, Dad."

He smirked, raising one eyebrow higher than the other, but he didn't say anything. He raised the book from his lap and reopened it. He cleared his throat and began reading again. Lou sat there thinking about apologizing for being rude. Before she did, he lowered the book enough for her to see his eyes again. They were smiling.

"Incorrigible," he said, and went back to reading.

Lou took that as a cue and slid her book from the stack. She hugged it against her chest, plodding through the maze of shelves until she found her favorite spot. It was tucked in the corner, to where she'd dragged an oversized fabric chair. She plopped into the chair, swung a leg over a curved arm, and cracked open the book.

She ran her fingers along the title page and then delicately turned the page. By the end of the afternoon, she was on the final chapter, *The Use of Spies*, for the third time. She didn't find that chapter especially useful. She couldn't imagine a time when she'd need a spy or become one. She flipped back a few pages to chapter twelve, *The Attack by Fire*. She traced her finger underneath the rule she thought best applied to her situation: *If it is to your advantage, make a forward move; if not, stay where you are.*

Her father had employed this rule since the Scourge cut her family in half. They'd stayed in one place until it no longer became safe; then they moved. It was frustrating for Lou; the uncertainty of their lives, the gnawing dread in the pit of her stomach always reminding her that everything in the new world was temporary. She thought about how much life she'd lived since her mother and brother had died. She wasn't the same person anymore. They probably wouldn't recognize her.

She closed her eyes, her finger still on the page, and tried to picture her mother's face. She couldn't. Not really. All that formed was a vague image of a woman's face. Lou couldn't quite sculpt its shape or size. How far apart were her mother's eyes? Was her nose wide or thin? Were her lips thin or full? How did they curl when she smiled?

She couldn't see any of it and remembered even less about her brother. But the smell of their bodies on the pyre? That was burned into her memory.

She jumped in her seat when a hand touched her shoulder. Her eyes popped open and she gasped.

"Sorry," said David, "I didn't mean to frighten you."

She exhaled and the tension eased from her body. "It's okay."

"What do you think?" he asked. "You've been at it a while."

"I've read it three times. You're right. It really is about the best way to avoid war. It's about doing everything possible to keep the peace."

"It's the same as the fundamental tenet of martial arts. Power should be used as a defense. Exercising force is a last resort, when all else fails. I want you to think about that."

Lou closed the book and set it in her lap. She understood that this was another "one day I'll be gone" lecture.

"There will be plenty of opportunities to strike first," David said. "It's not always wise."

"Okay."

"Think through every strategic possibility before you take it," he added. "Of course, it's not always feasible to do these things. But patience is your friend. Discretion is your friend. Peace is your friend."

"Now you sound like a character in *Shōgun*," Lou said. "James Clavell would be proud of you."

"I'm sure he would be. Wait, when did you read that?"

"Between a pair of James Michener novels," said Lou. "*Texas* and *The Drifters*. They seemed appropriate."

Her father smiled and rubbed the top of the cap on her head. He turned to walk away and stopped. He locked eyes with her and the smile melted away. He was serious now. He shook his head and swallowed. "I love you, Lou. I'm proud of you."

Lou's chest suddenly felt heavy. "I love you too, Dad. And I'm proud of you."

He winked at her and turned. He'd taken a few steps and was about to disappear around the other side of the bookshelf when she cleared her throat.

"Most of the time," she said with a sly grin. "I'm proud of you most of the time."

CHAPTER 16

DECEMBER 28, 2037, 4:00 PM
SCOURGE +5 YEARS, 2 MONTHS
KILLEEN, TEXAS

Lou was locked in the director's office reading Tolstoy when the glass shattered. She looked across the room at her father. He'd evidently heard the noise too. It wasn't her imagination.

"They're here," he said. "Turn off the lamp. Stay quiet. We'll be fine."

Lou wondered if they'd be fine. For weeks now, they'd been locked inside the library. They'd barricaded the doors as best they could, and they'd stayed hidden as much as possible from the advancing enemy.

Lou had wanted to act. She'd wanted to scare them off. Her father had thought better of it.

"They'll leave eventually," he said. "There's nothing here but that pond out front. Once they drink from it, clean up, get some sleep, they'll hopefully move on."

They hadn't. Three men had grown to five. Five had grown to ten. They'd circled the library countless times, looking for a way inside. Apparently, they'd grown tired of waiting and created their own entrance.

Lou's father hustled to the solar control panel and turned it off. He then hit the switch that provided latent electricity to the lights and appliances in the building. He didn't want them knowing there was a working refrigerator or microwave. That would only invite them to stay. He'd turned off the water the day the group had grown to ten.

The rumble of their intrusion grew louder as they ransacked the place. Lou could hear the men grunting and talking to each other. She inched closer to her father, leaning her body against his. She wasn't so much scared as she was anxious. Her heart pounded. Her tongue was thick in her mouth. Her neck and shoulders ached with tension.

"Do you think they're ruining books?" she whispered. "I don't want them to ruin the books."

A loud crash signaled what Lou assumed was a toppled bookshelf. There was clanging, which was almost certainly coming from the break room, which wasn't far from the director's office.

"I don't think they're here for books," David whispered back to her. "They want food and weapons."

A brusque voice bellowed from the hallway outside the office. "Hey," the man called. "There's food in the kitchen and the fridge is cold. It's like somebody was here."

The thunder of a responding horde followed the announcement, and the men crowded into the kitchen. Lou could hear them. They sounded like ravenous dogs as they tore through the remaining stores of food they'd kept in the fridge and in the cabinets above the sink.

Lou balled her fists. Her jaw set. She wanted to attack them now. She wanted to stop them from stealing what she and her father had worked so hard to procure. David must have sensed her desire to pounce. He wrapped his arm around her and squeezed her arm.

"It'll be okay," he told her. "We'll be fine. We can always get more food."

The invasion lasted for another hour. They'd tried the locked door of the office, but for whatever reason didn't try to break in. As they left, the men discussed staying inside the library but chose to leave.

They were comfortable in the elements. They could cook their food and bathe in the pond.

Although Lou thought they were stupid for leaving the library, she was thankful for that stupidity.

Over the next couple of days, a stray intruder would wander into the library and rummage through the kitchen or hunt the stacks for a book. Other than that, the men stayed outside, camped around the pond that separated the library from the road.

Lou and her father would sneak from the office at night. They'd gather what was left of their supplies from a hidden stash, use the restrooms, and check the security of their home. As each night passed and the food supply shrank to nothing, Lou knew they'd be leaving soon. They couldn't stay.

It had been more than five days when Lou's dad informed her he was going hunting. She'd protested. She'd begged to go. She was smaller; she could avoid the men and more easily hide from them.

"No," her father had said. "You're not going. I'll sneak out the back. They won't see me. I'll find a couple of squirrels or a possum. Then I'll be back."

"How long?"

"Less than a day."

"Hurry," she'd told him.

He'd kissed her goodbye and slipped out the back of the library and into the courtyard. She'd watched him, her nose pressed to the glass, looking outward this time. What had been her home now felt like a prison, and she was relegated to solitary confinement.

She'd waited patiently for him to return. She'd readied the knives for skinning whatever he brought back, and stayed hidden in the office. Then she heard a roar of laughter from outside and her stomach sank. Her fingers tingled, bile rose in her throat, and sweat formed on her neck and behind her ears. Something was wrong.

Now she stood against the window at the front of the library. It was dark outside, but the men had a large fire glowing at the edge of the pond. They were gathered around it, their forms flickering red and orange from the flames. Smoke poured from the fire, billowing into the cool air. Lou pressed her hands against the cold glass.

The crowd of men gave way for a moment, and she saw someone on their knees in the middle of the circle. His hands were behind his back. His head was down. Men took turns punching and kicking him. The man didn't react, he just took it.

Lou couldn't make out the man's features. She couldn't see his eyes or the shape of his face. There was no way to tell what exactly he was wearing. Everything was cast in shades of fire. But she didn't need to recognize any of those things to know the man in the middle of the circle was her father.

As the realization hit her and the bolt of fear raced through her body, she moved to the glass door closest to her. It was shattered. Shards of glass still clung to the metal frame. She reached to her hips and wrapped her trembling hands around the grips of her knives. Then she stopped herself.

She thought about all of the things her father had taught her. He wouldn't want her racing toward him, consumed with fury and rage. It would get them both killed. She stood there, fighting the urge to scream, and sobbed as she watched her father's last minutes alive.

Lou held out a naïve, childlike hope that they would let him go. Frozen with a combination of shock, confusion, and suppressed anger, she saw them dangle a pair of squirrels in front of him. They were taunting him with the food he'd caught.

More than once, the men pointed at the library. Her father always shook his head and lowered it. Lou knew what he was doing. He was protecting her, telling the men he was alone.

Maybe for his apparent candor they'd exile him from the college campus but let him live. Lou didn't know if he'd be able to walk, given the beating he'd sustained, but he'd crawl to freedom if he had the chance. Lou sniffed, realizing she couldn't breathe through her nose. It was full, as were her eyes. Tears streaked down her cheeks.

Her sweaty palms dampened the glass window.

And then, without warning, her father raised a fist and landed a solid punch square in the groin of the man closest to him. As that man doubled over in agony, another raised her father's rifle, the Mossberg that had kept them alive for so long, and pulled the trigger. The muzzle flash came first, but it didn't register. It wasn't until a split second later, when its familiar crack shook Lou's body and she saw him slump to the ground, that she knew what had happened.

Her body recoiled and she grabbed her stomach. She bit into her lower lip, trying not to cry out. Her chest heaved and she stepped back from the window, stumbling through the dark library, trying to keep herself from hyperventilating.

There was no reason to kill him. He'd done nothing to them. They'd already taken his food and his weapon. They could have left him alone. But they didn't.

She collapsed into her favorite chair, pulling her knees to her chest and hugging them, trying to force the flash of her father's death from her mind. She couldn't. It kept playing over and over again like a looping video. Lou knew her father would want her to escape, to quietly sneak away and make a life somewhere else. In the throes of her grief, through the fog of the sharp, agonizing pain that coursed through her, she already understood what she had to do.

She'd make a life somewhere else, that was certain. She couldn't stay here, not without her father.

But she wasn't sneaking away either. She was exacting revenge. Chapter nine of *The Art of War* taught her *if in the neighborhood of your camp there should be any hilly country, ponds surrounded by aquatic grass, hollow basins filled with reeds, or woods with thick undergrowth, they must be carefully routed out and searched; for these are places where men in ambush or insidious spies are likely to be lurking.*

She was the insidious spy. She was lurking.

***

Lou stood, checking the peppered holes in the books at her chest and the shallow wounds on her arms. She steadied herself, feeling the adrenaline wane, and stepped to the dead man. She stood above him and then squatted to look into his fixed, distant gaze.

"I'm my father's daughter," she said. "His name was David. My name is Lou."

She exhaled and pulled off her cap. She wiped the sheen of sweat from her forehead with the back of her arm and then heaved the book jacket from her body. She carried it in one hand, dragging it along the ground, until she reached the smoldering remains of a campfire.

She dropped the jacket and then dropped to her knees. Beside her was the dead body of her father. She reached out and tried rolling him over onto his back. She wanted to look at him. His body was stiff and resistant to her efforts, but she managed with a couple of heaves to move him. She inched closer to his face and cupped both sides of it with her hands. She closed her eyes and bent down to kiss his forehead.

As she drew back, she looked at him. He appeared different than she'd imagined he would. He appeared at peace. His eyes were closed and he carried the faintest hint of a smile.

Her eyes moved along his body, stopping at the trio of wounds in the center of his chest. She hadn't noticed at the time, but they must have shot him multiple times. A knot grew in her throat and she tried to suppress it. It didn't work. Tears welled and she silently sobbed over her father's body for five minutes or ten.

When she was finished, she removed her pack and set it on the ground. Then she moved around her father's head, stood, and took both of his wrists. With every bit of strength she could muster, she dragged him away from the other bodies and closer to the remains of the fire.

She walked back to the book jacket and picked it up, slinging it over her shoulders like a shawl, carrying it across the top of her back. She returned to her father's body and gently laid the jacket across him. She separated the books from one another, stretching the knotted fabric in a grid. It was made for her, so the jacket didn't cover much more than his torso. It was enough.

Lou walked over to one of the dead men and found a half-empty bottle of mash. She popped the top, sniffed it, and winced at the strong odor. She carried the bottle over to her father and emptied the contents onto the book jacket.

She tossed the bottle to the side and took a couple of steps to the smoldering fire. Picking up a stick, she stoked the embers until the flames reignited. It wasn't much, hardly more than a flicker. She walked around the other side of the fire, putting it between herself and her dad. Then she pulled a blade from her hip and shoveled some glowing embers onto the end of the steel. She held them there and then flicked them the short distance onto the soaked jacket. They sizzled but didn't catch. She tried it again and they took.

A carpet of blue flame spread across the book jacket and undulated for a moment before it bloomed into a healthy fire. The book covers turned black, their pages burned and curled. Then her father's clothes caught and, like her mother and brother before him, his earthly being was enveloped in fire and smoke. Lou stood there, as she had in her backyard more than five years earlier, and considered her future as much as her past. She thought about all the things she hadn't said, all of the times she'd put him in danger. She stood there, the familiar acrid scent filling her nostrils and stinging the back of her throat, blaming herself for his death.

Had she been strong enough to insist she go with him or hunt without him, he might still be alive. She didn't understand why, of all of the people she'd ever loved, she had to outlive them all. It felt like a punishment. Lou sank to her knees, letting the smoke drift into her eyes, accepting it as penance for her sins. She didn't know where to go or what to do. Her father's words echoed in her mind.

"I won't always be here to protect you. You need to learn to protect yourself."

Then Lou remembered what she'd told her father as he blamed himself for what had befallen their family in the early days of the Scourge. She remembered being the voice of reason, or comfort.

"I should've kept Davey home from school," he'd said. *"Then he wouldn't have gotten sick. Your mother wouldn't have—"*

Lou had held her father's hand with both of hers. She'd squeezed. *"Dad,"* she'd said, *"don't."*

Lou steeled herself, trying to swallow the self-pity that threatened to consume her. She moved away from the flames and picked up her pack, heaving it onto her shoulders. She rummaged through the belongings of the dead men, searching for anything useful. She left the guns. She had little use for them. If she couldn't get herself out of a jam with her knives, it wasn't worth surviving. She wasn't thinking clearly.

Fueled by newfound resolve but still clouded by grief, she walked away from the library and headed aimlessly away from her home. All she took with her was the pack, her knives, and the knowledge her father had spent the last five years drumming into her.

She swung the cap around on her head and found the highway leading out of town. It was early morning; the sun was almost ready to rise. For Lou, it was the first day of the rest of her life.

CHAPTER 17

SEPTEMBER 4, 2038, 4:00 PM
SCOURGE +5 YEARS, 11 MONTHS
EDEN, TEXAS

Six months or twelve, Lou wasn't sure how long she'd been on her own. She didn't keep track of days or weeks anymore. There wasn't a point. She had no agenda, nowhere to be, nobody to meet. She vaguely counted sunrises and sunsets, but after a couple of dozen she always lost track. Days didn't mean what they used to mean, not when subsistence was all that mattered.

She'd trudged from one abandoned ranch to another, empty town to empty town, always careful to avoid trouble. She was a scavenger, a coyote, who lived on whatever she could find or steal.

Lou wondered if anybody else in the forsaken wilderness of Texas was as lonely as she was. Was there anyone who was isolated, had nobody with whom to talk, share ideas, laugh, cry? She guessed there had to be somebody out there who was isolated.

Somebody. Somewhere.

She thought this as she sat perched about ten feet off the ground in a scrub oak. Waiting. The tree was a dead, or mostly dead, tree whose gnarled limbs were bare of leaves and looked almost like an old man raising his hands to the heavens asking for some sort of help from above.

It was nearly dusk and she'd been tracking a pair of oblivious men for more than two days. She was waiting for the right opportunity to pounce. First, she'd followed them long enough to make sure they weren't good guys. She had her internal set of loosely followed rules, one of which prohibited attacking, robbing, or otherwise harming good people.

These two weren't good. They were former Cartel. If their lame shotguns hadn't given them away, their conversations had.

Lou had stayed close enough to them that when they'd camped at night, she'd overheard them talking about the "good ole days" when they were in charge, when they didn't have to worry about Dwellers or the random smaller gangs popping up every day. They used to run with the confidence that nobody would mess with them. Now they confided to one another over a poorly constructed campfire that was more smoke than flame that they feared being attacked or harassed without fear of repercussion. The Cartel no longer had any power. It didn't elicit fear behind which it could rule.

One talked about the time he'd terrorized a family for more than a week while he and a band of grunts pillaged their homestead outside La Grange. The other tried to one-up him with a pair of stories about deadly confrontations with well-supplied ranchers unable to defend themselves against the numbers of grunts descending on their land. They spoke of trysts with women who weren't altogether consenting, lamenting the lack of underage women available to them now that the Dwellers had disbanded many of their favorite party spots.

Lou's jaw tightened, her muscles stiffened, as she listened to their conversation. They spoke as if their evil deeds were nothing to be ashamed about. They were not good men, not by any stretch, and it took everything in her to resist the swelling urge to leap from her hiding place amongst the weeds and kill them, with prejudice, immediately. But she slowed her pulse by breathing evenly through her nose. She closed her eyes and tried to picture something soothing, a waterfall or the slow wave of an overgrown field against a southerly breeze blowing in from Mexico or the Gulf. She could wait; she had the upper hand.

Lou had expected to attack them that night, but the men had taken turns sleeping. There wasn't a viable opening. She would be patient. As long as they didn't know she was shadowing them, she could take as long as she wanted and choose the exact right moment to ambush them.

She'd seen an opportunity when they stopped at a small muddy pond that was as much muck as it was water. She was behind them and on the opposite side of the dirt road, shielded by five-foot-high weeds and drought-resistant vegetation that thrived in west Texas. When they stopped, Lou carefully plodded ahead of them. She moved for nearly a half mile, finally sidestepping her way onto the road itself once she'd crossed a rise and fall in elevation that made it impossible for the duo to see her. She shrugged off her pack and dropped it onto the center of the dirt road, positioning it such that the men couldn't help but see it.

Then she climbed the tree and sat in the neck between the thick trunk and a forked branch that stretched skyward at forty-five degrees. Given that it was late afternoon and the sun would be in their eyes as they walked toward her, she figured there was no way they'd see her. If they did, they wouldn't be able to distinguish her from the tree.

They, on the other hand, would be lit perfectly. The sun at her back and shining on their faces would make the targets simple enough.

Lou checked the rise. No sign of the men yet. She had about two hours until nightfall. At that point, she'd lose her advantage. They still wouldn't be able to see her, but she wouldn't be able to see them either. That would complicate things.

"C'mon," she muttered. "How long does it take to do whatever needs doing at a mud hole?"

She had one knife in each hand. She ran her thumbs along the tops of the matte black metal handles where they met the hilt of the blades. They were so comfortable in her hands they felt as though they were an extension of her being. Lou and her knives. The knives and Lou. Since her father's death, they'd become a personification of her will and deadly determination. She'd even considered giving each of the knives a name. But she thought better of it, deciding that only lunatics and losers named their weapons. Anyone who took the time to name a weapon—a gun, a knife, a lasso, a throwing star—was someone who was a card short of a full deck. She was as certain of that as she was about anything else in her uncertain world.

She balanced the knife in her right hand at the end of the handle and flipped it up in the air. It spun twice and landed in her hand as it had left it. She flipped it again, tossing it higher. Three revolutions later, it was up, down, and back in her grip. Then she closed her eyes and tried it. Perhaps it was careless. If she dropped the blade and it tumbled to the ground, she could lose her advantage. She'd have to climb down to get it and, by then, the duo could be over the rise and spot her.

She knew that wouldn't happen. She flipped the knife upward. It spun rapidly four times before returning to her hand. She smirked to herself. It was a bemused smile, one that said, "Yeah, I can do that."

She repeated the test with her left hand. By the time she'd caught it a fifth time, ready to try both simultaneously, a stolen glance at the horizon spotted the tops of two heads.

The men were on their way.

Both were roughly the same height and walked with nearly identical gaits. She wondered if they were related. Cousins? Brothers? They'd never made mention of a family connection, but as they approached, she couldn't help but think they were somehow kin. Neither of them was very tall; both were slim. Even from a distance, Lou could tell they weren't much bigger than her.

Both of them had shaggy brown hair. It was remarkable only in the sense that most men had shaved their heads or kept the cuts close cropped. The Cartel, she'd heard anecdotally, had forced many of the grunts to do this to cut down on disease and to dehumanize them, to make them function as a collective instead of individuals. But many other men not in the Cartel had followed suit. It had stuck even after their fall and the rise of the Dwellers.

The two weren't part of the crowd. Their clothing was further evidence of it. Most wore tattered, used clothing that fit awkwardly if at all. Men cinched their pants with belts or ropes. Women wore frocks that were either too tight or hung like draperies. In the post-apocalypse, everything was a hand-me-down.

These two wore khaki pants that, while stained, fit them well. Their shoes, brown canvas, were in good condition. Their long-sleeved black T-shirts were faded gray, but hung nicely at their collars, and the arms stretched all the way to their wrists.

Lou steadied herself in the tree, nestling against the trunk for balance as they drew closer. She locked her eyes on the one to the left. He was holding his shotgun in his hands. The other had it stuffed into a pack on his back. Its stock poked up from behind his head at an angle.

They were talking to each other and not paying much attention to the road ahead. They certainly weren't looking at her. She readied herself, the familiar anticipatory tingle rippled through her body, and she exhaled slowly. The men were within ten feet when she raised her arm, flicked her wrist forward, and spun the knife into the target's neck. He grasped at the blade. His mouth open and closed like a fish, a reaction she'd seen before, and he stumbled backward. Incredibly, as Lou watched in amazement, the man pulled the blade from his neck and held the knife in his hand. He stared at it before his eyes rolled back and he collapsed onto the dirt with an unceremonious thud. He dropped the shotgun at his side and fell onto it.

His unexpected reaction, which had held Lou's attention for a beat too long, had given his companion time to react. Before Lou could wing the second blade at him, the second man quickly wielded the shotgun, took a giant step forward, and unloaded two loads of shot toward the tree. While he was too far to hurt Lou, the twin booms knocked her off balance. She fell backward from the crook of the branch and the trunk, catching herself before she tumbled to the hard, root-scarred ground below.

The man unloaded another blast as he cursed at her, questioning who she was and why she'd done what she did. Lou couldn't answer him. She'd dropped her second knife and was clinging to the back side of the trunk with a bear hug involving her arms and legs.

He raced toward her as she slid down far enough to jump safely to the ground. The rough bark of the scrub oak scraped painfully against her soft palms as she hurried downward. But she landed on her feet as another blast, this one much closer, sheared bark from the edges of the tree and sent splinters darting through the air like exploding shrapnel.

Lou searched the ground for the knife. She didn't see it. A fourth shot shattered the air. He was only a few feet from her, but Lou still had the advantage of the low, bright sunlight that offered her some protection. She ducked instinctively at the percussion of the blast and, as she did, spotted the blade. She dropped to her knees and scurried a short distance toward it. As she spread out, landing chest first onto the ground to reach the knife, the protruding tentacle of an oak root caught her such that it knocked the air from her lungs. She gasped futilely, thinking for a split second she'd been shot. She rolled over onto her back in time to see the man standing over her. His legs were spread shoulder width apart. His shaggy hair draped across his eyes. He aimed the shotgun at her face. Lou froze, her eyes locked on his, and the man didn't hesitate. He pulled the trigger.

Click.

His eyes widened and he lowered the shotgun to check it. He fumbled with it, giving Lou enough time to suck in a breath, exhale, and reach for the knife.

She blindly grabbed the handle while on her back and rocked forward as she flung it at the man. Her aim was low and it sank into his thigh. It wasn't fatal, but he did cry out in pain and dropped the shotgun as he reached for his leg with both hands.

He stayed on his feet, hobbled, and seemed to consider pulling out the blade. He stood there, grimacing and gripping both sides of his thigh.

Lou got to her feet and dove headfirst into his stomach, knocking him off balance and onto his back. He grabbed onto her as they fell, and grappled for her neck. Lou found the blade handle with her right hand, withdrew it from his leg, and hammered it two more times into the same spot.

The man lost his grip on her, and she took the knife, flipped it around in her hand, and stabbed it into his chest, using all of her weight to punch it downward, finishing the job. She held it there as he flailed weakly underneath her before sliding it out and rolling her body off his.

She blinked up at the sky, still trying to fully catch her breath, and listened to the faint gurgle leaking from his open mouth. There was a rattle, a final push of air from his lungs, and he was quiet.

Lou closed her eyes and replayed the fight in her mind. If his shotgun hadn't misfired, she'd be the one dead on the ground. She bit down on the inside of her cheek, angry that she'd put herself in such a precarious position. It was avoidable. She'd been the aggressor, however patient, and had almost bit it.

Once she'd caught her breath, she rolled onto her stomach and got to her knees. She inched over to the dead man and shoved him onto his side. She pulled free one of his pack straps, pushed him again, and yanked off the other one.

Lou dragged the pack against the tree and trudged over to the other dead man. He had an identical bag, which was equally as heavy. After retrieving her knife and wiping it clean on his long-sleeved shirt, she yanked the pack from his back and dragged it along the dirt back to the tree. She leaned against the oak and slid down the side, sitting against it. She rubbed her chest where the root had punched her. She winced from the bruise and tried stretching back her shoulders to ease the discomfort. Lou thought of Sun Tzu.

Bring war material with you from home, but forage on the enemy. Thus, the army will have food enough for its needs.

Lou unzipped the first of the two packs, opening it wide. She reached inside and pulled out a pair of socks, then another pair. There was an older first aid kit with a broken hinge on the box, a utility knife, some strips of dried meat tied together with a string, and a half-empty bottle of water-purification tablets.

She shook the bottle of tablets and set it to one side, next to the socks, and untied the strips of meat. Holding a piece up to her nose, she sniffed it. It smelled okay, though she couldn't tell what kind of meat it was. It didn't matter. She was hungry. Killing a man could do that.

She tore a piece of meat off with her teeth and chewed. It was gamey. Not the best. At least it was protein and might give her the energy bounce she needed to walk through the night.

Lou picked up the bag and dug into it up to her shoulder, groping for anything else that might be in the pack.

There were spare shotgun shells rolling around loosely at the bottom of the bag. She fingered the shells out of the pack and held them in her open palm.

She glanced at the dead man closest to her. "You could have used these," she mumbled. "They didn't do you a lot of good in the bottom of your bag."

"You're right," she said, affecting a deeper, male voice. "If I weren't an idiot, you'd be the dead one right now and I'd be going through *your* stuff."

She returned to her voice. "Funny how life works, isn't it?"

"Or doesn't," she replied to herself in the deeper voice.

Lou's eyes drifted from his face to his feet. They were small. She slid her heels toward the dead man, setting her soles against his. His shoes were a half size bigger than hers. Not much more. She scooted forward, her rear end bumping against the exposed tree roots, and reached out for his canvas shoes.

She unlaced one at a time and examined them. They were in much better shape than her boots, which had seen better days. The rubber soles of the canvas shoes were solid, without worn holes, as she had in her boots.

She hastily pulled off the boots and tried on one of the shoes. It was too loose, bigger than she'd thought. She cursed the shoe and then spotted the extra pairs of socks she'd set on the first pack. She unrolled a pair and slid them over the stiff, soiled pair already on her feet.

She slid the first shoe back onto her foot. It fit. Lou excitedly drew the second shoe onto her other foot and laced both, double-knotting them at the top. She hopped onto her feet and walked a bit, trying the feel of the new shoes.

She smiled. "I'm guessing this is what Christmas feels like," she said aloud. She vaguely remembered the holiday, but given how sad the good memories of her mother and brother tended to make her, she'd pushed most of them into a vault at the back of her memories.

She spent the next hour consolidating her existing belongings with her newly acquired loot. She traded her smaller pack for one of the larger, more efficient packs the dead men had been wearing. Atop the back of the pack, written in neat lettering with a black marker, was a name: McCarty. She had no way of knowing if McCarty was the man she'd killed or if he'd taken it from someone else. It didn't matter, really. McCarty's pack belonged to her now.

She slugged it onto her back and adjusted the straps to fit her. It was heavier than what she'd been carrying, and it dug into her already worn shoulders. Yet she could manage.

The sun was about to dip below the horizon. It was sinking faster now and the sky was a fiery red at its edges. It blended into a deep purple before the dark, deep blue that spread across the majority of its broad expanse.

Lou was ready to hit the road. She still didn't have a plan. There was no place in particular she needed or wanted to be. Still, she had to keep moving. Of that much she was certain. Unlike the scrub oak that had been the centerpiece of her afternoon, she refused to be rooted to one place. It hadn't worked out too well for the tree, which was brittle and living its final days. Its roots, the very things that gave it life, were also what were slowly killing it.

Lou sucked in a deep breath of the cooling air and knelt in front of the shoeless dead man. She turned him over onto his back and grabbed his jaw with her hand to turn his face toward her. She stared into his eyes. His body was already starting to stiffen.

Their color was dull and milky. They were vacant and stared right through her into some distant place he couldn't quite focus on.

Lou studied each of his eyes, their shape, the way they were set into their sockets. It was something she'd chosen to do with the last ten or twenty men she'd killed in the last year. There was something about the ritual that helped her rid herself of the guilt she always felt in the moments after she'd listened to a death rattle or winced at the shrieking agony a victim endured in his final seconds on earth.

She'd resolved to do this after considering the alternative. Lou couldn't allow her guilt to consume her. She was a good person, she knew that. At least she forced herself to believe it. She chose her targets carefully, only attacking those she believed worthy of her wrath.

Looking into their eyes was cathartic. It was if she'd purged the person, and the world, of their evil. That evil, so often evident in a person's eyes, wasn't there when they died. She knew, from reading books about anatomy, that when a person died his muscles relaxed, causing the pupils to dilate and grow large. But in the hours after death, when rigor mortis began to take hold, the muscles constricted and the pupils shrank. Sometimes, as she'd observed firsthand, one pupil would remain larger than the other. The shapes of the eyes, in death, might differ.

Studying the eyes was a way to make the killing clinical, something that could allow her to remove the guilt. She chose to believe she was committing an act of preemptive self-defense.

This shoeless man had matching eyes. Both pupils were shrinking. The shape had remained the same. Lou quietly prayed for his soul and for hers. It wasn't that she was a believer—her life experience had left her relatively devoid of that kind of faith—but she wanted to believe in some higher power, some karmic being who would set right the bad and reward the good. Lou didn't know where she fell on that pendulum. She tried not to think about it except in that moment where she measured a dead man's eyes in the minutes after she'd stolen the life from him.

A breeze had begun to swirl around her as the sun disappeared beneath the horizon. It rustled through the high, grassy weeds on both sides of the road. It was as if that karmic being was whispering back to her. Lou turned to watch the tops of the weeds undulate like fields of wheat. Tears moistened her eyes and she blinked them away, wondering what the cosmos truly thought of her.

What would her dad think of her? That was even more important.

Would he be proud she'd survived or disappointed in the way she'd chosen to make it happen? She'd become a hunter to avoid being prey. A swell of red-hot anger boiled in her gut. If she wasn't good, if she was a disappointment, wasn't that what he'd taught her to become?

She wiped her eyes dry and adjusted the pack on her back, tucking her thumbs underneath the padded shoulder straps. As the red faded into purple and then to black, she marched ahead. Her new shoes felt good on her feet.

CHAPTER 18

A dusting of snow covered Highway 281 near the Colorado River. Lou was transfixed by the path ahead as a shower of flakes drifted from the gray sky, landing on her cheeks and the backs of her hands. It was the first time in her life she'd seen snow. She only knew what it was because she'd seen pictures of it in an encyclopedia and read about Dickens's description of it in *A Christmas Carol*.

Scrooge, she remembered, had been unaffected by anything around him, including the wintry weather and the snow. As she walked across a bridge, heading north, she couldn't imagine how anyone, even a fictional character, couldn't be excited by snow. She wanted to jump and skip. Her eyes moved from the road to the flocked trees, the powdery white riverbank, and the countless flakes that danced in the air, swirling and blowing in all directions. Its collection on the bridge itself, a thin layer of accumulation, was magical.

The beginnings of the snowfall had awakened her three hours earlier than she'd planned to rise. Over the last few months, she'd gotten back into the habit of sleeping at night and traveling during the day. Moving at night had become more precarious given the exponential rise in regionally organized gangs.

There were no more Dwellers per se, and the Cartel was almost a distant memory. But in any lawless society, as was the case south of the wall, the good people ceded control to the bad. The gangs, almost without exception, tended to do the bulk of their business at night. Lou adapted her habits to avoid them as much as she could. Every once in a while, she'd cross paths with a desperado intent on stealing from her, or worse, and she'd be forced into action.

On occasion she still would instigate the altercation and violent exchange of goods. She was hardened. She was the cynic her father claimed she had become. Her wicked sense of humor had gotten her into pickles more often than it had saved her from them. Post-apocalyptic Texans apparently didn't enjoy sarcasm the way she thought they ought.

Lou was, in every sense of the word, an adult whose sole purpose was survival. There was no joy. There was little laughter for the sake of it.

And so, when the predawn wake-up call of icy flakes of snow had landed on her face and instantaneously melted, a sense of wonderment stirred inside her she had long forgotten she was capable of feeling. She'd risen from under the bank of yaupon trees about twenty yards from the highway on the outskirts of Marble Falls, confused about her opaque surroundings. As soon as she'd understood it was snowing, she quickly pulled herself from her hand-sewn canvas sleeping bag and readied herself for the day's journey.

She crossed the bridge and tilted back her head, opening her mouth wide and catching the flakes on her tongue. She giggled, and then giggled more at the surprisingly girlish sounds she was making.

Her breath puffed in large plumes in front of her face as she slid her canvas shoes along the asphalt. Every few steps she'd spin around one hundred and eighty degrees to look at where she'd been. Other than the sound of her feet on the road, the only sound was the breeze swirling around her. The air even smelled different to her. It was damp but clean, a refreshing odor absent the dust that hung low and settled on everything.

Her fingers were red with cold, her nose was wet, and the tops of her ears stung. But she didn't focus on any of it. She flexed her hands, wiped her nose, and pulled her cap lower on her head. She delighted in the experience.

A three-hour hike felt like it passed in thirty minutes. The snowfall had intensified by the time she'd reached her destination. She barely recognized it.

The coating of white on the roof and the undisturbed carpet up the long driveway made the property unfamiliar. She had to check the address stenciled onto the curb to make sure she had the right place. She did.

Her heart rate revved as she walked along the driveway to the front of the house. Her hands, long since numb from the cold, tingled with a disconcerting combination of anticipation and nerves. Her mouth was suddenly dry. She stuck out her tongue to catch some snow and rolled the melt around inside her cheeks.

She reached the front door and balled her hand into a fist so as to knock on the door. Before she did, the door swung open. A frail man stood there, his body trembling. She didn't recognize him, but he immediately knew her.

"Lou?" he asked. "Is that you?"

She nodded and stole a glance over the man's shoulder into the house. "Teddy?"

An awkward smile appeared on his face, revealing swollen gums that no longer held teeth. He smacked his lips. His hands and arms trembled as he extended them for a hug.

"My goodness," he said, his voice warbling in concert with his shaking body. "You've grown."

His eyes lifted from hers and scanned the yard. His eyes narrowed and he looked at Lou with an expression she recognized as pity.

He wrapped his arms around her and she reciprocated. She could feel his ribs and his shoulder blades straining against his skin under his thin sweater.

He backed away from her and motioned her inside. She crossed the threshold and ducked inside the house. It was only moderately warmer than the outside. It was dark, and there was the distinct odor of ammonia.

Lou stood in the small foyer and waited for Teddy to lead her to the living room in the back of the house. He shuffled past her, using the wall for balance, wheezing as he moved. When he reached the living room, he rounded one of the sofas and sank onto it, using the wide arm to lower himself gingerly onto the plush seat. He sank deep into the worn cushion and leaned back. His fingers danced on the arm as if he were playing the bongos.

Lou shrugged off her pack and set it on the floor by the back windows. The snow stretched all the way to the river. The bank was wider now. The water level was a good two to three feet lower than she remembered. She stood there for a moment, her back to Teddy, remembering the countless days she and her father had spent on the water fishing for dinner. She didn't turn away until Teddy broke the silence.

"Earlene's gone," he said. "Got sick about a year ago. Pneumonia or the flu. Not sure. She went fast."

Lou pivoted on her heels and faced him. She looked down at her shoes, unable to look him in the eyes. "I'm sorry," she said softly.

"I miss her," he said. "She was a strong woman. She was my backbone."

Lou didn't know what to say. "I'm sorry," she repeated.

"No need to be sorry. All of us die eventually. We start dying the minute we're born. It's how the world works."

Lou lifted her chin. "You're not sad?"

He chuckled. His body was still shaking. "Of course I'm sad. She was my reason for living. I miss her awful. Plus, her cooking was so much better than mine."

Lou crossed the floor and sat on the sofa opposite Teddy, bouncing on the misshapen springs in the cushion until she got comfortable.

"I've got Parkinson's," he said. "I know you can tell. It's okay if you stare. It's an odd thing, really. My body shakes all the time. Wears me out. Makes it hard to relax. Sleeping isn't easy neither."

Lou swallowed hard. "Dad's gone."

Teddy frowned. "I figured as much. You showing up here all alone, I guessed he wasn't around any longer."

He didn't say he was sorry, but the sudden glisten in his eyes told her he was. She couldn't be sure the welling tears were for his wife, his illness, the world, or her dad. It didn't matter. It was nice to sit quietly with someone who could empathize with the depth of loss she'd experienced when her only companion had left her alone in the world.

After several minutes of silence, Teddy's expression changed. His eyebrows arched and his eyes widened. "How about the snow? Kind of a miraculous thing. I haven't seen snow in I don't know how many years. Earlene would have loved it."

Lou looked out the window. The snow was still falling. There was a good couple of inches on top of the picnic table out back. "My dad would have loved it."

"I'm guessing he would have," said Teddy. He stared past Lou, out the window. "There's a blanket behind you if you're cold. Earlene knitted it herself."

Lou pulled the blanket from over her shoulder and stood up. She carried it over to Teddy and draped it across his lap. Then she sat next to him and put her hand on his.

His hand was cold, his rough skin marked with age spots and purple with veins running close to the surface. It trembled, like a constant vibration, underneath hers.

Lou wasn't sure why she'd done it. She hardly knew Teddy. Her father and she had spent hardly a day with him, and Earlene had done more of the talking. But there was a connection she couldn't explain, a magnet that drew her back to the house so many years after she'd left.

Teddy and Earlene were two of the few people with whom she and her father had had meaningful contact since the Scourge. In that way, Teddy was her lone surviving friend.

He squeezed her hand. "Why'd you come back?"

Lou exhaled, her gaze still fixed beyond the picture window at the snow. She could see her breath. It was that cold in the house.

"I don't know," she said. "I felt like it, I guess."

"What have you been doing all this time? It's been, what, five years? Six?"

Lou cupped his hand with both of hers. "About."

"How long since your dad—"

"I lost track," she cut in.

There was a lilt in his voice when he responded. "Oh."

She rubbed the back of his hand. "Sorry. I didn't mean to sound rude. I really don't know. Sometimes it feels like it happened yesterday, and other times it's like it happened in another dimension, a long time ago."

"A galaxy far, far away."

Lou looked at Teddy with confusion. "What?"

"Nothing." He chuckled. "It's an old movie reference."

"They killed him," Lou said. It was the first time she'd ever said it aloud.

"The Cartel?" he said softly, the warble in his voice more pronounced.

"Them or the Dwellers. I don't know for sure. It doesn't matter. They're dead too."

Teddy didn't say anything. Then he slowly pulled his hand away from Lou and set it in his lap. Lou shifted on the cushion, the springs creaking, and she looked up at Teddy's face.

His head was shaking. His shoulders shuddered. His chin quivered. But his eyes were as clear as they'd been since she'd arrived. They were sharp and focused on her.

The soft look of pity or empathy was gone. In its place was a grim expression, his lips pursed and twisted to one side of his face. His brow was furrowed with concern, and a deep trio of vertical creases ran between his eyes. He stared at her disapprovingly, in a way she suddenly remembered having seen on Earlene's face when the woman first realized Lou had been living in her home uninvited. He shakily lowered his chin and eyed her hip.

Lou followed his gaze and noticed the knife handle sticking out from underneath her thin jacket. There was a smudge of dried blood along the trim of her coat where the handle rubbed against it. Then she watched him take stock of the pack over by the window. Written in marker across the top was the name McCarty. He looked back at the knife and then into Lou's eyes.

Teddy pushed himself from the sofa and feebly walked to the other side of the room, close to the doorway that led to the kitchen. He leaned on the door frame. The expression on his face hadn't changed except that the concern had deepened.

Those three words she'd muttered offhandedly, as if it were of no consequence, had changed everything in a split second. Teddy knew who she'd become, though he didn't know her well enough to understand why.

"I think you should go," he said. "I'll give you some food if you need it. But you can't stay, Lou."

Her throat tightened and a heaviness pressed down on her chest. Her gut churned. She couldn't speak. If she did, she knew she'd cry. That would only make things worse.

He held up a finger. "Stay there. I'll be right back."

Lou sat there on the sofa, upset with herself for having said anything to him about her father. She shouldn't have opened up. That was a mistake. Now he thought her a ruthless killer, which was only partly true. For all he knew, she was there to kill him.

Lou pressed her hands flat on the edge of the sofa and stood up. She crossed the room to the window and grabbed her pack. She heaved it onto her back, grunting softly, and stared through the frosty glass. She could feel the cold leaking through the single panes.

The snow had slowed. The flakes were smaller now. They still swirled and danced as they painted their way through the air before adding to the thickening accumulation on the ground.

Lou wished she hadn't come here. She should have known better. What did she expect to find? Earlene with a warm pot of fish stew and a big smile? A warm house she could call home?

She leaned into the window, getting lost in the rush of the low-flowing river, the gently swaying trees on the opposite bank. She sighed and turned away from the glass at the same moment she heard the familiar double-slap pump of a shotgun.

Confused, she reached for her blade. Then she saw Teddy standing in the kitchen doorway, leaning against the frame and shakily gripping the weapon. Its muzzle was dancing with his inability to hold it steady.

Lou raised both hands in surrender. Tears streaked down her cheeks.

"I need you to go," he said, vaguely motioning toward the front door. "I can't have a killer living here."

Lou swallowed against the painful swelling in her throat. "But, Teddy, I—"

"There's nothing you can say, Lou. I don't care whether you were getting revenge or whatever. I could see it in your eyes when you got here. You're a killer. You're one of them coyotes out there in the wilderness, scavenging and stealing. You'll do whatever it takes to stay alive."

He was right. She would.

"I'm sure you're a fine girl and all, but truth be told, all I know about you, when I think about it, is you lived in my house by breaking in. Then you come back with blood on you and somebody else's bag. You're desperate, Lou. I can smell it on you. You can't stay here."

He was right again. She *was* desperate. What he didn't understand was that her desperation was for human contact, for conversation with someone other than herself.

Keeping her hands up, Lou backed away from the window and walked around the far side of the sofas. She kept her eyes locked on Teddy. Through her tears, she watched him motion repeatedly toward the door.

As she moved into the foyer, he shuffled into the living room so he could keep the weapon trained on her. He was too far away at this point to do any harm. It didn't matter. Lou wasn't staying, and she wasn't challenging him.

She hesitated at the door, one hand on the knob, and sucked in a ragged breath. It was cold and stung as she inhaled.

"I wouldn't hurt you," she said.

She didn't wait for a response. She walked through the door and shut it behind her. She trudged through the snow, crossing the yard instead of taking the driveway. Her feet crunched on the snow and buried ice. She tucked her hands into her jacket pockets.

The cold air on her tear-streaked face stung. When she reached the road, she turned back the way she'd come. Her shoe prints were partially buried in new snow, but she could see them. She tried matching them as she walked, making a game of it to distract herself.

Not once did she look back at the house. Even when she heard the door creak open. Even when Teddy called her name. Even when he asked her to come back, telling her he'd overreacted.

She didn't want to be with someone who couldn't understand what she'd been through, why she'd done what she'd done, and how she'd become the person she was.

CHAPTER 19

JUNE 2, 2041, HIGH NOON
SCOURGE +8 YEARS, 8 MONTHS
ABILENE, TEXAS

"You're ugly," said Lou. She held a knife in each hand. Her thumbs rubbed along the edges of the ergonomic metal handles. "And you stink."

"Are you trying to get shot?" asked the greasy, mannish woman standing across the room. Her hair was cut short and parted to one side. The part was severe enough to reveal a thick, straight line of pale scalp from the crown of her bullet-shaped head to her brow.

It was true. The woman *was* ugly. And she stank. Neither of those observations were up for debate. When they drew a chuckle from the others in the bar, Lou was certain the woman would draw the pistol from her hip and unload its six rounds in her general direction.

Lou knew the same could be said for her, actually. She was covered in a sheen of dirt, and the summer heat had produced a disgusting lather under her arms. If she were honest, she probably couldn't distinguish her stink from anybody else's.

"I'm not trying to get shot," she said, standing with her feet shoulder width apart. "I'm just calling it like it is."

The woman, Laura Bullion, wasn't part of a gang, but she was an outlaw. Lou had heard of her in other parts of Texas. But not until today had she met her face to ugly face.

Bullion was a gambler and a cheat. She was also a quick draw and not opposed to using her feminine attributes to get herself out of otherwise sticky situations.

Looking at her now, Lou wondered why any man would be interested in her. It wasn't as if she had a sparkling personality to offset her horse teeth, hawk nose, and wide-set eyes that looked like they were about to pop under pressure.

"Only reason I haven't killed you yet," Bullion snarled, "is 'cause I don't make a habit of shooting children."

Lou didn't like being called a child, which happened a lot because of her slight build and baby face. She wasn't about to correct Bullion though. She took stock of the others in the room. There were twelve people, including herself and the barkeep. The barkeep was harmless.

So that meant there were ten people she had to worry about. Most of all, at the moment, was Laura Bullion.

"You ever read *Cyrano de Bergerac*?" asked Lou, staring at the woman's nose. "It's a French play."

There were two other women in the room. One of them had been playing cards with Lou and Laura. The other eight were men, three of whom were part of the game.

"What's that got to do with anything?" asked Bullion. She stood at the table, her chair toppled behind her. She leaned on the table. "What do you want, girlie?"

"I want what I won," said Lou. Her eyes darted around the room and landed on the pot at the center of the card table: two cans of beans, a sealed box of rice, a length of rope, and a bottle of sour mash.

Lou wouldn't drink the moonshine, but she could sell it for food, weapons, or survival gear. She'd won the game. She'd counted the cards. The face cards in all four suits had been played. Somehow, though, Laura Bullion had managed a one-eyed Jack to beat Lou's hand.

Lou had called her on it. That had started the standoff in the middle of the bar. Three of the men were armed, as best she could tell. Other than Bullion, none of the women were.

"Last time I checked, two jacks beat a pair of nines," said Bullion. "Do I have that wrong?"

Lou scanned the room. Everyone was frozen, even the armed men with the grizzled faces and strong jaws. Even the women, who looked like kind, motherly souls. All of them kowtowed to the cheating gambler with the quick draw and the lethal reputation.

"I won that hand," said Lou. "You know it; I know it. Everybody here knows it. They can smell it. Or maybe that's just you they smell."

Bullion's eye twitched. Her fingers tapped on the side of her holster. She glanced at Lou's hands, and Lou wondered if she'd gone too far.

"You know you brought a knife to a gunfight," said Bullion.

Lou licked her cracked lips, raking her teeth across the loose, dead flakes of skin. "I brought two."

Bullion chuckled, her lips peeling back to reveal her wide gums. She did look like a horse, minus the tail and friendly disposition. "Tell you what, I like your spunk. How about we split the pot? That fair enough?"

The offer surprised Lou. She tried not to let it show on her face. Bullion had no reason to make the gesture. She *did* have the gun. For all Lou knew, some of the others in the bar were with her.

Lou spent three seconds considering her offer. She shook her head. "No," she said. "It's not fair. You cheated. You pulled a jack from your sleeve or somewhere else. I won the pot. I want all of it."

The equine grin evaporated from Bullion's face and she shrugged. "All right then. I'm gonna have to take it all."

At that moment, when Lou thought she'd pushed it too far, the door to the bar swung open. A large man in a brown hat announced a holdup, pumped his shotgun once, and blasted Laura Bullion, who was closest to the door, in the chest.

Laura's grunt and squeal were muted by another blast. The other women in the bar and some of the men dropped to the floor, screaming in fear.

Two more men emerged from the bar. They too opened fire.

Lou pushed the card table onto its side, facing the door. The loot and the cards went flying, and she dove behind the wooden table for cover. She didn't recognize the men in the doorway. The brown hat meant nothing nowadays. It was identical to the ones Cartel posse bosses had worn, but there was no Cartel, and there were no posse bosses. Chances were he'd stolen it from someone who had stolen it from someone else.

Lou stayed low as the cacophony of gunfire thundered throughout the bar. Two of the men in the bar had returned fire before being gunned down where they knelt. As Lou took in the scene, trying to get her wits about her and figure out a way to survive, a bloody hand grabbed her wrist and yanked her toward the floor.

It was Laura Bullion. She was lying on her side in a spreading pool of blood. She gripped Lou's arm tightly with one hand and offered her the pistol with her other. Her face was devoid of color, and her gums, pink and healthy a moment ago, were gray.

She mouthed something Lou couldn't hear or understand. She tucked away her knives and reached across Bullion's body to take the pistol. It was a six-shooter, a Smith & Wesson .38 Special identical to the one her father had carried. It was heavy in Lou's hand, but lighter than she remembered. It had been years since she'd wrapped her palm and fingers around the molded grip. She mouthed a thank-you to Bullion and rose up to take aim.

The hat-wearing man with the shotgun was reloading. The two other men, one with a rifle and the other with a pair of Glocks, had their attention elsewhere. Lou wrapped both hands around the grip and pulled the trigger. The weapon kicked and her aim was high. Since she'd been trying to tag him in the chest, the round slugged him in the cheek instead. A second shot was truer and hit him center mass. The man with the shotgun collapsed where he stood.

Lou dropped back behind the table and curled herself into a ball. She'd gotten lucky with the first man. The other two wouldn't be as easy.

The barkeep managed to wing the man with the twin Glocks. He dropped one of the weapons and it skittered across the floor, landing at the feet of an unarmed mustachioed man with long fingers and a cleft chin. He didn't hesitate to pick up the handgun and fire. He unloaded the magazine and hit his target three or four times. It was enough to kill him.

The last man standing was the one with the rifle. As Lou rose up from behind the table to meet him with the .38, he backed away from the fray. Still popping shots, he ducked out through the front door. The echoes of gunfire still rang in Lou's ears. Moans and cries for help grew louder. She scanned the room. Of the twelve people she'd counted during her standoff, eight of them weren't moving. Two of them were injured. Only Lou and the barkeep appeared unscathed.

Anger welled inside her and she pushed away the table. "I'll be back," she said to the barkeep and marched out into the bright, white-hot sunlight of midday.

She turned left and then right before seeing the rifleman hurrying away. He was about fifty yards from her. His back was to her, and he was limping.

Lou steadied herself and took the weapon in both hands. She stood with her legs spread, her body leaning over her feet. She called out to the man, "Hey! You forgot something."

The man turned, slowing just enough and giving her a wider target. She applied steady pressure to the trigger and fired.

No sooner had she released the pressure than she pulled the trigger again. And then a third time.

The first shot missed the target. When he turned away from her, the second one hit him squarely between the shoulder blades. He lurched forward, stumbling, until the third shot hit him in the lower back, and he flopped forward onto the street. He dropped the rifle. The side of his head hit the asphalt with a crack.

Lou turned around and walked back into the bar. The bartender was helping one of the wounded. The other one wasn't breathing anymore. She picked her way through the room to the table and crouched behind it in front of Laura Bullion.

The woman was still alive, though barely. It wouldn't be long. Minutes. Maybe seconds.

Kneeling, Lou found Bullion's distant, cloudy gaze. She smiled at the cheat and took her cold, bloody hand. Then she pressed the Smith & Wesson into it and laid it on her chest.

"Thank you," she said to the woman. "You saved me."

Bullion's eyes jerked to one side and then the other, as if she were trying to find Lou but couldn't. Then she inhaled one final time and took her last ragged, bubbling breath.

Lou reached over and took the pot, stuffing all but the mash into her pack. She slung her pack over one shoulder and carried the bottle to the barkeep, handing it to him. "You can use this more than I can."

The bartender took the bottle with a weak smile and went back to working on the only other survivor of the holdup. Lou smiled back and walked away. Once again, she was in the sunlight.

Lou stood in the street for a moment, staring at the small crowd of people that had surrounded the dead rifleman. She watched them pick through his pockets and remove his shoes.

She glanced back toward the bar and thought about Laura Bullion. Even in a woman with a mean streak a mile wide, there was good. Nobody was all of one or the other. Good people had their bad; bad people had their good. It was on a sliding scale. Lou knew that. As she walked away from Abilene with the hope she'd never go back, she wondered if she'd ever find anyone who was the perfect balance of both. Was there anyone she could accept and who could accept her?

"Someday," she muttered to herself. "Someday."

CHAPTER 20

OCTOBER 21, 2042, 6:32 AM
SCOURGE +10 YEARS, 19 DAYS
EAST OF RISING STAR, TEXAS

Lou heard him before she saw him. He was walking on the cracked road that passed as Highway 36. She wondered if he was part of the Llano River Clan or any of the other nasty-minded gangs that had been gaining power and influence.

She had done her best to avoid them when they traveled in larger groups. If they rode in pairs or trios, she would occasionally ambush them and take from them what she could. The last she'd seen any of them was outside Abilene a couple of weeks earlier. She'd avoided that group. They'd looked especially hardened and ready for a fight.

She'd gotten good at spotting the ones to skip and the ones to engage. There was a way they walk or rode that gave them away. How armed they were also played a role. The more loaded for bear they were, the more likely she was to keep a low profile and let them pass.

When she saw this lone ranger, in silhouette against the deep red of dawn, she sensed there was something different about the way he carried himself. There was a definite confidence in his stride, an aura of danger that surrounded him like a warning sign. Yet there was also a sadness in the way he walked. Lou couldn't place exactly what it was, but he definitely wasn't LRC.

The sun was behind him as he trudged westward. It was low on the wavy horizon, barely tempering the coldest part of the day. He carried a bolt-action Springfield slung over his shoulder, a large pack strapped to his back, and he carried a semi-auto in his right hand.

As she stalked him, she took note of his appearance. His hair was cropped short and matched the scruff on his cheeks, chin, and neck.

He passed the low-slung building on his right, his eyes scanning the adjacent empty lot, his index finger on the semiautomatic's trigger guard. She wondered if he could sense her presence as he stopped at the Dairy Queen on the corner of 36 and South Main.

Lou darted behind the old police station and hid behind the building. Her pulse quickened. The thought that he'd spotted her was both terrifying and exhilarating. She considered letting him pass, but he was a loner. She couldn't help herself. He was too easy a mark.

He kept moving as though he hadn't seen her. If he'd known she was there, he'd have already taken a shot or two, wouldn't he?

He kept his gaze forward, his gait the same, as he trekked through the town. He'd moved past Avenue E near the 7-Eleven.

Lou darted across the space between two buildings, her canvas shoes slipping across the gravel, and that was when she knew he'd made her. He quickly moved off the road and crouched behind a rusting gas pump under a dilapidated metal awning. He swiftly slid the Glock into his holster and looped the rifle strap over his head, shrugged the backpack off his shoulders, and placed it on the ground in front of him. He lay down on his stomach, legs splayed for balance, and rested the rifle on the pack. Within seconds he had one eye to the scope and the Springfield ready to fire.

Lou froze in place for a moment on the right side of the building. It wasn't often she was surprised by an opponent's actions. Like a good chess player, she was always thinking a dozen moves ahead. Her pulse was pounding now. She wiped her sweaty palms on her pants, moving her feet. She froze again.

He'd spotted her. No doubt. When she'd moved her feet, he reacted. It was almost imperceptible, but there was a change in his posture. She thought she might have even seen him smile. If he was any good with that rifle, she was toast. Then he gave her an opening.

He twisted his body and looked behind him toward the empty, weedy lot that stretched for most of the block. Lou bolted to the middle of the store, crouching low behind a rusting shelving unit. She skidded to a stop and tried to catch her breath. This was a much better spot. He wouldn't see her here.

She squatted with her behind resting on her heels. She shifted her weight, using her hands to balance herself. That was a mistake.

The shelving unit creaked and its base scraped against the concrete floor, emitting a loud screech. Lou cursed herself under her breath and regained her balance. She reached for her knives, making sure they were tucked in her waistband.

"Hey!" the man called. "I don't want to kill you, but I've got you in my sights. My finger is on the trigger."

His voice echoed in the cool morning air, reverberating off the valley of abandoned stores and houses. Holding her breath, Lou listened to the echo.

"You'll have to come out eventually," he said. "Might as well save us both some time and do it now."

Lou weighed her options. She didn't have any. She could keep hiding; he'd eventually light up the place and she'd be dead. She could step out into the light and he could take her out before she had a chance to react. She let go of her breath and looked behind her. There wasn't a clear path to the rear exit. There were obstacles everywhere. Even if she managed to navigate the uneasy path to the back door, he'd have a clear shot at her. Then again, if he'd wanted to shoot her, he would have already done it. Maybe he did just want to talk. If that was the case, perhaps she could regain the upper hand. He'd see a little teenage girl emerge from the debris like a rat. It would disarm him, if only for a second. That could give her the opportunity to take aim.

She peeked out from behind the rack and raised her hands above her head. She narrowed her eyes, trying to gauge the man's intentions.

He lifted his head and stole glances to either side of her. "Who's with you?"

Lou stepped forward, awkwardly maneuvering around the debris in the store. With her hands above her head, she moved from the store to the parking lot, her brown canvas shoes crunching on broken glass.

He tapped the trigger guard with his fingertip. The rifle rested on the pack, its business end aimed at her. He tracked her with it as she moved closer. She focused on the weapon, careful not to change her expression. The last thing she wanted was for this loner to sense fear.

"Are you alone?" he asked.

Lou lowered her hands, her arms loose at her sides. She wiggled her fingers as if playing a concerto on an invisible piano. She tilted her head from one side to the other, cracking her neck, without taking her eyes off the man. She could tell he was measuring her, gauging if she was a threat.

The man sighed. His shoulders sagged. "You need to—"

Sensing the infinitesimal lowering of his guard, Lou moved quickly. Ignoring her father's—and Sun Tzu's—sage advice, she acted. With incredible quickness, she drew a knife from behind her back and flung it at the man's head. The sunlight glinted off the blade as it hurled toward him. As soon as it left her hand, she knew her aim wasn't true. The knife whipped past his head and harmlessly nailed a wooden utility pole right behind him.

The man jerked his head away from the knife's path and slid his finger to the trigger, but he didn't fire. "Hey," he said sternly, as would a father scolding his disobedient child, "put your hands up now. Both of them over your head. Or I pull this trigger."

Lou frowned, upset with herself for the errant throw, and raised her hands. She rested them on her ball cap and laced her fingers.

"Stay put," the man ordered. "One stupid move and you're toast. Do you understand?"

She didn't acknowledge him as he stood and approached her with the rifle aimed at her chest. "Do you understand English?" he asked. "*¿Habla Español?*"

Lou shrugged. She wasn't about to say anything. Let him guess. Keep him off balance.

"I don't want to hurt you," the man said. "Do you understand me? Can you understand what I'm saying?"

Lou understood him. There was a hint of a Texas drawl in his voice. He was a trim man who clearly hadn't let the apocalypse get the better of his fitness. Most people, Lou had noticed, were either grotesquely thin from malnutrition or overweight from a lack of motivation. This man was neither. His muscles strained against his shirt, his neck was thick, his jaw was squared. His face was in the early stages of weathering, the hints of crow's-feet at his eyes and the shallow etch of a frown line on the inside of each cheek.

His eyes revealed the most about him, however. Reflected in them was the experience of a man who'd seen things he couldn't forget. There was wisdom there. And there was pain. So much pain. Lou recognized it because she'd seen it before. She'd seen the unenviable mix of experience and hurt in her father's eyes. Every day since the Scourge, it had been there. For some time after her mother's and brother's deaths, the wisdom had succumbed to the anguish. It had hidden behind it. Only time had helped experience reemerge.

The pain in this man's eyes was still fresh. It ran deep.

He adjusted the rifle, tightening the stock's position against his shoulder, and motioned to his right. "Turn around."

When Lou hesitated, he jabbed the barrel at her. "Now," he barked.

She turned around, her back to him.

"I'm taking the knife," he said.

Lou braced herself and waited for him to touch it. When he did, she spun, grabbed his wrist, and twisted it.

The man responded with skill. He backed up and pulled hard, yanking Lou off balance enough that he regained control of the knife and wrestled it free from her as she struggled to stay on her feet. He moved quickly away from her, the knife in one hand and the rifle in the other.

"You've got fight," he said. "That's good. It'll keep you alive."

Lou wiped her face with the back of her hand. Her chin was tilted toward her chest, and she looked up at him angrily through her curtain of hair.

She was breathing through her mouth, her jaw slack. Her chest heaved and her tattered shirt hung from her body. Her fingers were curled into fists.

The man sighed and limped backward toward his pack. Lou hadn't noticed the limp before. If she had, she might have taken a different tack. She cursed herself again.

He retreated in a defensive but ready posture. Still facing her, he crouched down, wincing at the pressure on his leg, and snatched up his pack. He slung it over one shoulder and backed onto the road. He stopped at the utility pole and levered the knife free of the wood.

"You dropped your hat," he called, and turned to resume his march away from her.

She hadn't even noticed the cap was off her head. She felt her matted hair and then spotted the Astros hat, her father's hat, on the ground. She picked it up, rubbing the rim with her fingers.

"You can't take my knives," she called out to him. "I need them."

He glanced at her over his shoulder and kept walking.

"Can I please have my knives?"

"Why? I give you the knives and you'll kill me with them."

"I promise I won't," she said, mostly meaning it, and added a charming Southern twang to her voice. She hoped it might make her appear simple and less cunning. "I ain't got nobody, just me and my knives," she added.

He looked west and then back east from where he'd come. The sun cast a hazy glow in what was now a pale blue sky. A bird flapped overhead and then glided toward a cluster of scrub oaks on the northern side of the highway. The man clenched his jaw.

"We're in a no-win situation," he said with the hint of a smirk on his battle-worn face. "I give you the knives, you wing one at me and stick me in the back as I walk away. I take the knives and you probably don't last a week out here."

He was right. Absolutely right.

Lou lifted the hat and set it on her head, spinning the brim to the side. She fingered her hair from her eyes, pulling it back across her shoulders, and shrugged.

"How long you been out here alone?" he asked.

She lowered her eyes. "A year or two. Could be longer. I stopped counting."

"What's your suggestion?" said the man with a paternal tone that somehow lacked condescension. "You're smart. What would you do if you were me?"

Lou smirked and she took a step closer. She had an idea. "How about you leave the knives in the pole there," she said with her false accent. "Jab 'em real good. I stay where I am, and when you're far enough away, I get my knives. You go your way and I go mine."

He glanced at the utility pole and then back at Lou "That doesn't help me out. You tried to kill me."

"There are bad people out there who need killing," said Lou, pulling back the curtain on her own experience and pain. "Hard to tell them from the others sometimes."

The man ran his fingers along the twin knife handles tucked at his waist. "You're right about that. We don't know enough about each other to know whether either or both of us need killing, right?"

Lou figured the question was rhetorical. She didn't answer.

"Let's figure it out," he said. "I can't leave you here to die if you're the kind that needs to live, but I can't give you your knives if I'm the kind that needs to live. So how about I keep the knives for now, you tag along with me, and I keep you fed? We get to know each other, and at some point, we'll figure each other out."

Lou reflexively wiggled her fingers at her sides, recalling the comforting grip of the blades. "And then I get my knives back?"

"Depends on what kind of person you are."

She huffed. "Or what kind *you* are."

"Exactly. I'm heading west to Abilene."

Lou adjusted the cap on her head, her eyes widening with uncertainty. She wasn't fond of the idea. "There are bad people in Abilene."

"There are bad people everywhere," he said, shrugging the pack higher on his back and starting to walk away.

Lou sighed. She couldn't lose the knives. She hustled to catch him, which wasn't hard given his slow pace and his limp. Her stomach growled.

"You said something about food," she said. "You got water?"

The man unhooked the canteen from the side of his pack and handed it to her. Lou uncapped it and gulped, streams of water trickling down her cheeks. It tasted good. It felt good.

"Not too fast," Marcus said. "You'll get sick."

She took another large gulp, storing it in her cheeks, and handed back the canteen. What was left of the water sloshed around the inside. The man drew it to his mouth and slugged a mouthful. He swished it around in his mouth and curled his cracked lips around his teeth, moistening them.

"We're gonna head north in a bit," he said. "We'll camp for the night. There's a lake south of I-20. We'll hit it by nightfall."

Lou bobbed her head and fingered her hair behind her ear, tucking it away from her face. The man slid the knives along his waistband to his right, away from her. She should be angry at him, angrier than she was at herself for having been outsmarted, but she wasn't. In his face, behind those eyes, within that resonant Texas-barbed voice, was something comforting. Maybe it was that he reminded her in some small way of her father. Maybe it was the pain he carried. She empathized with it. She understood it. Unlike so many who wore their lack of good fortune as a chip on their shoulder, this man strapped it to his gut as motivation. True, he had her knives; that wasn't good. But he hadn't retaliated when she'd attacked him. That was good. That said more about him than all of those other things that made her trust him.

He was going somewhere. He was on a mission. She didn't know what it was, and she didn't care. She walked behind him, paying attention to his limp, watching his pack bounce on his strong back. The sun rose at her back, casting her shadow in front of her. But it wasn't just her shadow she chased. There was another one just ahead of her. As they walked, the morning grew warmer, a yellow hue cast across the dry, dying landscape. The road ahead looked golden in the light. If she squinted her eyes, it was ethereal and made her think of L. Frank Baum's most popular work. She wondered to herself which of the characters she would be: the Tin Man in search of a heart, the Scarecrow hoping to find a brain, or the Lion in want of courage. She dismissed them. She had a heart, a brain, and more courage than men twice her age. She was Dorothy, the heroine in search of a home. Then again, she wasn't sure the world had any heroes left. It was merely full of survivors, some of whom were more cunning than others. The man walking in front of her had plenty of cunning to go along with his skill and his evident kindness.

It didn't really matter who was who on the journey to Oz. For all she knew, the man was Dorothy and she was Toto. What mattered was that she'd unwittingly found a companion, for however long it lasted.

ACKNOWLEDGMENTS

I'll start this one by thanking you, the fans. If it hadn't been for the incredible reception Lou received in RISING and in BATTLE, I don't think telling her backstory would have occurred to me. Thank you. I hope you got what you wanted. Maybe someday, she'll return in a new story. Maybe.

Thanks to Steve Kremer and his wife Nancy. They've been ardent supporters and Steve has been an incredible resource through all of The Traveler Series and The SpaceMan Chronicles.

Major props to my "team" of professionals who make the schlock I crank out on my Mac and turn it into something special. Felicia Sullivan always gets first crack at shaping the stories into coherent narratives. She's incredible and brutally honest. The same is true for proofreaders Patricia Wilson and Pauline Nolet. They fine tune the work, making it sing in tune. Stef McDaid, at Write Into Print, does yeoman's work and always supplies first-rate formatting for the digital and print copies. And then there is Hristo Kovatliev. If you could judge the book by the covers he creates, I'd be much better at what I do. He's a genius.

Of course, my family is always behind me. They encourage me and give me time to write. They're magnificent and generous in a way that humbles me. I love you Courtney, Sam, and Luke.

Thanks also to my viral marketers; my parents Sanders and Jeannie, my siblings Penny and Steven, and my mother-in-law Linda.

I'll stop there. It's time to write the next book.

Made in the USA
Coppell, TX
29 January 2025

45149532R00132